CYN VARGAS

ON
THE
WAY

STORIES

CURBSIDE SPLENDOR PUBLISHING

The stories contained herein are works of fiction. All incidents, situations, institutions, governments, and people are fictional and any similarity to characters or persons living or dead is strictly coincidental.

Published by Curbside Splendor Publishing, Inc., Chicago, Illinois in 2015.

First Edition
Copyright © 2015 by Cyn Vargas
Library of Congress Control Number: 2014959439
ISBN 978-1-940430-47-8
Cover images © Cas Cornelissen/Unsplash (spine); Florian Klauer/Unsplash (top cover); Allyson Souza/Unsplash (bottom cover and interior)
Designed by Alban Fischer

Tips for positions for pregnant women from Babycenter.com.

Manufactured in the United States of America.

www.curbsidesplendor.com

You know where you are with
Floor collapsing, floating
Bouncing back and
One day I am gonna grow wings

—RADIOHEAD,
"Let Down"

CONTENTS

ON THE WAY

GUATE

When I graduated eighth grade, Mom took me to Guatemala. It was the first time she'd been since she left at eighteen. She would often talk about it as a magical place with volcanoes that spurted lava, and black sand by the ocean. Mom thought I was finally was old enough to enjoy the country. I didn't know it would be the last time I would ever see my mother and hear her voice. I wish we had never gone.

At La Aurora International Airport, we rolled our bags past a throng of people who were holding flowers and balloons and stuffed animals. Mom's aunt, Blanca, was supposed to meet us there. I had only seen her in pictures. She looked like a raisin in each one, short and dark and wrinkled.

"There she is," Mom announced, taking my hand and leading me to her. Tía Bianca was even smaller than in the pictures. The bouquet of strange pink and orange flowers she was holding covered her face.

Mom and Tía Blanca hugged and cried. A man with a giant straw hat came up to me and asked if I wanted to buy some mangos or a machete. I understood Spanish, but didn't speak it well. I just smiled, shook my head and said, "Gracias." He nodded and walked away.

"Oh, you're so pretty," Tía Blanca said. She had learned English at college. Even though we were the same height, she wrapped me in her arms. Her sweater smelled like vanilla.

On the cab ride in, Mom pointed out special places she remembered. "You see the cemetery? Right there. They bury people above ground and then paint the tombs bright colors. Death is not to be mourned here. It's a part of life."

The cemetery was on top of a hill and the bright orange, blue, and pink squares looked like candy spilled from the sky.

"You see how the volcanoes look so close? They're really miles and miles away. That volcano there still is active and spits out lava. Now, look over there. That volcano is active, but instead of lava, it has water. It erupted a few decades ago and flooded the downtown area."

We swirled through the streets of Guatemala City, where there were so many honking cars it was like there were a thousand geese in the road. Tía Blanca fell asleep, her chin resting against her chest, hands folded in her lap. Mom held my hand, something we hadn't done since I was young. With the other, she pointed out more places—the school she had gone to that was just letting out, kids in blue uniforms running for freedom. She pointed at all the skinny stray dogs in the road, pointed at the street vendors: auto parts, bread, whole dead chickens hanging off a line, bananas, clothes, even goldfish. She smiled and squeezed my hand each time she said something.

"Selma, look," she said and pointed to a tiny shop with *Selma's Panaderia* scrawled across the window in black paint. "I used to go there every week to get bread as a kid. I said when I had a daughter, I would name her Selma."

The first week in Guatemala Mom and I were inseparable. We stayed with Tía Blanca in a house where she lived alone. She started calling Mom and I las gemelas, which made my mom laugh.

We shared a bedroom with a white fan and a bed covered with a loud, dandelion-patterned blanket, which was stitched in different places with various colors of thread. Every morning, Mom and I would walk in the street along the many makeshift booths, where generations of women dressed in Mayan clothes of patterned hues tried to make a living. We bought sweets stuffed with fruit, earrings made of feathers, and hair clips in shaped like flowers or bows that we used to keep our bangs out of our faces in the fierce sun. We paid with creased bills that were printed in the center with a beautiful green bird with a red belly and long tail that Mom told me had been hunted into extinction. We bought bracelets made from colorful beads, our names burned into a long wooden bead while we watched. Mom's was too small for her wrist but she still paid the lady, who had a baby sleeping in a sling across her chest. Mom gave her bracelet to me and I wore both hers and mine together.

I took pictures of Mom and Tía Blanca: my mom's arm over her aunt's shoulder, both of them leaning against the door of Tía Blanca's house. We went to the beach, where the sand was black and the ocean was clear. I took a snapshot of Mom in her swimsuit, standing in water up to her calves. She stared into the endless water, the rose tattoo on her thigh glistening. She had gotten it when I was little, and told me that the rose was just for me. In the summer, when my mom wore shorts, I would trace the rose's outline with my fingers while we watched cartoons. I'd tell her that when I got older I was going to get a tattoo just for her, too.

The last picture I took of Mom was of her sitting on the front stoop eating a guayaba, a stray dog with visible ribs sprawled at her feet. When I took the picture, she laughed and said, "Selma. How many pictures is that now? Two thousand in a week?" She raised her guayaba, the reddish orange pulp inside shining in the morning sun. The streets swarmed with cars, people, and even a couple of horses among the dogs.

"You feeling ok?" she said.

"My stomach hurts."

She put her hand on my forehead. "Well, you don't have a fever. Maybe it's something you ate. You didn't drink any milk, did you?"

I said nothing.

"Selma, I told you this is not like the States. Not to eat anything dairy."

She asked Tía Blanca, who was waving at some passing neighbors, to make me some tea and to make sure I lied down.

"I'm going to pick up some groceries," Mom said.

"Be careful, Adriana," Tía Blanca said, and went upstairs to boil the water.

"Don't go to the beach without me," I said, rubbing my stomach.

"When do I ever do anything without my twin?" She kissed my forehead and held my wrist. The bracelets rubbed against one another. "Go on up and lie down. I'll be back soon."

Her long curls swayed as she crossed the street. Her skin had darkened like toast in the few days we were there. She dodged speeding cars and slow dogs, turning when she got across to wave at me and point at the door of the house. I waved back. She smiled, and I could see her bright eyes, despite all the sunshine. She turned the corner into a crowd of morning chaos.

Later that afternoon, I woke up from my nap expecting to see Mom in the kitchen with Tía Blanca, drinking café con leche and eating the pastries we had bought that morning. But Tía Blanca was alone, her hands wrapped around a mug.

"Is Mom back yet?" I asked, feeling a little bit better.

"No. Not yet. Maybe the buses took long,"

she said, but the wrinkles across her forehead deepened, and continued to do so as the hours dragged on.

By sunset, Tía Blanca had called every family she knew who had a phone, which wasn't many. Then she called the police. An hour later, two pudgy men in gray uniforms arrived. They wore heavy badges that tugged their shirts down, and had matching thick mustaches. Tía Blanca sputtered that Mom was visiting from the States, that she had left for the store but should have been back hours ago. Then the men began to question me. "You an American? Why did you come here?" They asked about the jewelry Mom was wearing, and had I noticed anyone following us since we arrived. When they left, they took the only developed pictures of her that we had: the four we had taken together in a photo booth at the airport, printed on a single strip. In two of them we were making kissing faces, in one we were sticking out our tongues, and in another we were smiling, looking right into the camera lens. Tía Blanca kept crying, and I went to bed.

That night, I dreamt with her. Mom sprawled in her bathing suit on the sand that was as black as her hair. The rose tattoo, faded crimson with two green leaves that curled at the ends, sprouted from her hip. The waves were rolling in, almost touching her feet, which were pointed at the sky.

Without looking at me or moving her head, she said, "Selma." Though it was a whisper, I could hear her voice skimming the sand as it made its way to me. I smelled the wet sand and the coconut oil that she had rubbed on her skin.

"Mama," I said, though my lips were sealed shut and began to bleed when I opened them. I swallowed the blood that came through my teeth. It dripped down my chin and onto my bare feet.

"Selma." Mom turned her head toward me this time. The sun grew brighter and her skin began to sizzle. I could hear it, inhaled the smell of it. Her hair fell away at the roots, exposing her white scalp. Her eyes were shut. I began to cry red tears and ran over to her, but each step caused her to melt more. Her skin stank like forgotten meat. Her screams released into my veins.

I stopped running and she stopped dying, and when she called my name again, I didn't know if she wanted me to keep going.

It was strange to see Mom's picture on the news. The anchors spoke quickly. The reporter wore too much makeup and her concern didn't seem sincere while she spoke of the American that went missing. I wanted to reach into the television and yank out that picture of Mom and me at the airport. They only showed the frame where we leaned into each other, each of us smiling. I wanted my mother next to me again.

Tía Blanca was on the phone with Tía Carmen and my grandma in the States. I spoke to Grandma once, but all she did was cry and I didn't know what to say.

After a week, Mom was no longer on the news, and I was thankful. I hated those news anchors. They pretended to care, but when they switched to another story, they would laugh and forget all about her.

The room felt dreary even in the daylight. The sun highlighted the wilted flowers on the bedspread and layers of dust on the fan. At night it was worse. The bed was too big, the pillow next to me stiff, Mom's side of the bed untouched. I would stare for hours at the fan, hearing its drone, feeling Mom's bracelet I wore until I fell asleep.

In the mornings, Tía Blanca scanned the paper for news of Mom. Her hands shook.

"Mom's coming back, right?" I asked.

"I don't know. God said to never lie."

After two months, the police lost interest. Sometimes I'd hear Tía Blanca on the phone talking about an article she had read in the paper describing a body that was found. But it was never Mom. She caught me listening once, scrunched up the paper, and told me to go to my room.

We went around the neighborhood, passing out fliers with Mom's picture on them, but no one seemed to have any hope to give us. They just shook their heads and patted me on the back.

The volcanoes of lava and water both seemed to hide secrets from me. Every way I turned there they were, looming colossal in the distance. They were able to see everyone and everything, everything that happened before them. I wanted to beg them to tell me where Mom was.

One morning after mass, where Tía Blanca and I prayed and lit another candle, I said, "Mom is coming back, right?"

"No, she's not." She put her soft hand on my face.

We were blocking the entrance of the church. People squeezed by us. The bells rang. My heart strangled on her words.

"I would love for you to stay, but you need to go back home, Selma. You belong back home. Your mom would have wanted that."

"But Mom is coming back. I have to be here. I want to be here," I cried.

"I'm old. I can't take care of you. You're going to go stay with your Tía Carmen and your grandma in Ohio."

"I'll take care of you," I blurted, but I meant it. "I can't leave."

"She's not coming back, Selma. Please. You look just like her. I can't have you here anymore." She grabbed my hand and I wanted to pull away from her, but didn't. We walked in silence to her house.

"Tomorrow, a taxi will take you to the airport," she said, and unlocked the front door. "I'm sorry."

"But when she comes back—" I started to say. Tía Blanca turned to face me. Her sweater was torn at one elbow, her gray hair was sparse. I saw chestnut spots on her scalp. She seemed even older than when we'd arrived just two months earlier.

"Do you know what happens to pretty women that go missing here? Pretty American women? She's gone. Now, please." She said something more, but a sob muffled her words, and she went into her room and shut the door.

The next day, she made a breakfast that I didn't eat. She kissed me on the forehead and sat next to me in the taxi. My bag and Mom's were in the trunk. We didn't say anything. She looked out her window and I looked out mine. Tía Blanca wept softly. The city was busy as always, but I felt detached from it all. We drove past Selma's Panaderia and I began to cry. The taxi driver didn't say a word to either of us during the hour drive to the airport. Instead, he played some music that I knew Mom would've liked.

At the airport, Tía Blanca leaned over and kissed my head. She stayed in the cab when I got out. I didn't watch it drive away.

On the plane, I sat next to the window. On my other side, a fat lady slumped over and snored. I pressed my face against the glass and gazed at the green mountains and the ocean. I thought I could see Mom, fading away behind the clouds.

I waited outside the Dayton terminal with an airline employee who was dressed in all blue. "Have a good time on vacation?" he asked.

I didn't say anything. Tía Carmen was supposed to pick me up. I had only ever seen her at Thanksgiving and Christmas back in Chicago, when she would visit my grandma. Last year she hadn't come at all, since Grandma had decided she would rather live with her daughter in Ohio than in a nursing home in a big city.

A black car drove up and honked. Tía Carmen looked older than the last time I had seen her. Her curls were dark like Mom's, but with blonde highlights. She wore huge sunglasses even though the sun wasn't out. A neon pink scarf choked her neck. The employee patted me on the back and helped me put the bags in the trunk. Tía Carmen popped it open without getting out of the car.

"You should start grieving for your mother," she said as soon as I shut the car door. The leather seats were cold against my legs.

"What?"

"I said, 'You need to start mourning your mother.'" She drove with her left hand and punched the radio buttons with the other, shifting the music from Oldies to R&B to Spanish Rock. The rhinestones on her red plastic nails glittered in the evening sun.

"But Mom isn't dead," I said.

The car's heater wasn't turned on and I blew into my hands. I could smell Guatemala underneath my fingernails.

"She's dead, Selma," she said, as if I had just asked her the time.

"No, she's not." I turned to look out the window. Some kids in matching hats and gloves were making miniature snowmen in front of a house, their mother watching from the windows.

"Don't be foolish, Selma. She's been missing for months, and in Guate, of all places. She's dead, and the sooner you accept that, the sooner you can move on."

I didn't say anything. Mom used to tell me that by the time Tía Carmen came along, Grandma had run out of love to give her.

"I'm cold," I whispered, my voice low under the changing lyrics. Shadows cloaked our faces as we drove down streets with giant oaks and underneath viaducts. "She's not dead," I said again, a little louder. I blew breath onto my window and traced hearts into the fog. They faded as quickly as they appeared.

"You get to stay downstairs with your grandma," Tía Carmen said as we pulled into her driveway. The petite house had a square front window that was covered in snow. A weak light flickered in the basement window. Tía Carmen grabbed my bag from the trunk and walked in front of me. I rolled Mom's suitcase across the sidewalk, brushing off snow as it collected.

"Mom, be careful with those candles," Tía Carmen yelled as we walked in. The house was dark and cold. When she turned on the light, I saw that the mismatched loveseats and the fat TV were the only things in the living room.

"Your grandma's downstairs. Tell her to show you where the extra blanket is," she said. She pointed at a door whose frame had peeling white paint and hung from its hinges. "I'm working the second shift tonight. I made dinner. It's on the stove if you get hungry." And with that, she walked just a few steps into a room in the back and shut the door.

The house was silent except for the shower that had come on and a kind of humming. The door to the basement squealed a bit when I opened it, the wooden steps cried out under my feet.

I had spoken with Grandma over the phone every so often after she moved away, but I hadn't seen her in over a year. There was no light switch that I could feel, so I left my bags at the top of the steps. The humming got louder. The air smelled like roses. The flame of a red candle on a table quivered angrily.

At the bottom of the stairs, I saw Grandma's shadow, long and thin, stretched like gum against the wall. I couldn't tell what was her and what was her shadow.

"Grandma," I whispered, taking a few steps towards her. She was kneeling before a tiny basement window. The candle, thick and short, stood next to a picture of Mom in a yellow gold frame so large it seemed like the photo had shrunk behind the glass.

I realized that only Grandma's lips were moving as her fingers hurried the rosary through the transitions. I don't know how long I stood there. A door slammed and the lights in the driveway momentarily flooded the basement. Grandma kept on praying. She wore a red nightgown that matched the red candle. The clear beads of the rosary were pink next to her nightgown.

Then the headlights were gone, Tia Carmen off to work, and we were in darkness once more. After my eyes adjusted, I thought I saw Mom moving in the candlelight. When Grandma neared the large, metal cross that hung at the end of the rosary, she stood, and I heard her say, "Adriana."

Grandma flipped on the switch over her bed. I shut my eyes.

I opened my eyes. She sat on the edge of her twin bed. Her body shook as she cried. I saw on her feet the enormous, faded black slippers that used to be my grandpa's.

"I pray every day that your mother comes back to us," she murmured, her eyes wet and her weak hands in mine. I noticed the bags under her eyes. She hugged me, and her body felt impossibly fragile. She repeated Mom's name over and over while I stared at the photograph on the wall. I willed for it to move again.

"Selma, I know you didn't want to come, but I'm happy you're here." She took a blanket and pillow from the closet.

"I'm really tired," I said, but I wasn't really. I just didn't want to talk about it.

Grandma snored the whole night. I lay on a cot that stank like mold. I was supposed to be back in Guate, in Tía Blanca's house, so that when Mom came home she would see that I had been waiting for her. I wanted to hug her and kiss her and have her stroke my hair tell me again how I was taking too many pictures. I was supposed to be there, with a hot cup of café con leche and a pastel de fresa—her favorite, which she savored because they weren't as delicious in the States.

Instead I was lying next to my snoring grandma, thousands of miles away.

I watched Tía Carmen make eggs for lunch. Grandma was praying again downstairs. The rumble from the trucks that passed outside on the main street rattled the house.

"Can you get the orange juice?" Tía Carmen asked. I got up from the table and walked over to the fridge. A black and white photograph hung from the door: five little kids in spotless shorts and shirts and dresses. I saw the volcanoes in the background.

"That's your mom, right there." Tía Carmen pointed at the girl in an oversized dress. "And that cute baby she's holding is me. The other three are our cousins." She turned away again and the eggs sputtered in the pan. Mom looked happy; all the kids did.

"I don't have any kids 'cause I never wanted any," she said, setting two plates of eggs on the table. We sat down. "That being said, Selma, you can stay here 'til we figure all this out. Your mom and I were close once. Not for many years, but that doesn't mean I didn't love her." She grabbed her fork and played with the eggs. I did the same.

"Your Tía Blanca told me how you didn't want to leave. How you think she's still alive. You need to accept that she's gone. They would have found her by now." She took a sip of her orange juice. "Your mom's landlord sent over some of your stuff. It's in the garage. He said he sold the furniture for the rent money you guys owed him for the time you were in Guate."

After she left to run some errands and Grandma lay down for a nap, I went into the garage and found a few boxes with *Adriana* scrawled across the cardboard in red ink. They were full of her clothes and some jewelry. I also found her album of photographs of only the two of us. We had planned to fill with pictures from our trip.

That night, Tía Carmen came home with a letter. She opened it in front of me and then quickly stuffed it in her purse. She glanced at me and forced a smile. While she slept, I did something Mom would have grounded me for. I dug into Tía Carmen's purse and found the envelope. I went into the bathroom and turned on the faucet. There was a note from Tía Blanca, and an article clipped from a Guatemalan newspaper. The note from Tía Blanca read, "Carmen, this is the one I was telling you about. They have found more. Not her though."

The paper was already turning brown. It was in Spanish, so it took me a long time to read it. It said bodies of women had been found in a rural part of Guatemala. There was a photograph of some policemen standing over a body covered in a white sheet. The woman they found had blonde hair. I stuffed it back in the purse.

That night when I had a nightmare, Grandma hummed and caressed my head 'til I fell back asleep.

A month later, Tía Carmen enrolled me in the high school down the street. By then, she had purchased me my own twin bed that I put in the basement. At night, Grandma told me stories of Mom growing up. How when she met my dad she was happy, and how devastated she was when he left us both.

"She loved him, but she loved you more. Know that," Grandma said once.

I made a few friends in high school, but I lied when they asked about my mom.

"Her company has her working in Guatemala right now," I said and the other kids thought that was cool.

"You must miss her," a girl told me once. It took everything not to cry.

Tía Blanca began to call me every other week.

"Please forgive me," she said in our first call.

"It's alright, Tía," I said. Her voice was like
Guate calling to me, asking me to return.

I developed the last pictures Mom and I took
together in Guate and put them in the album.
Often, I would look at them while going through
her suitcase filled with her clothes. Both stayed
right next to my bed where I could reach out and
touch them.

Tía Carmen kept getting articles in the mail. I
could tell when she'd get one because she'd rush
into the house, throw the rest of the mail on
the counter and scurry into her room, clutching
her purse. Later, I would find ripped pieces of
newspaper in the trashcan, too shredded to make
anything out.

When Tía Carmen wasn't working two shifts, we
all ate breakfast together. On Sunday we went to
church, and even though none of us said so, I
knew we were all praying for Mom.

"I pray she comes back soon," I said once in
the car driving back home. I was in the back
seat and saw Tía Carmen and Grandma give each
other a look.

"Selma, she's gone. It's been a long time," Tía Carmen said, and glanced at me through the rearview mirror.

"Grandma, you still think she's coming back, don't you?"

Grandma lowered her head to her hands.

Tía Carmen pulled the car over next to a public park. I could hear the kids in the park screaming and laughing as they played.

"How about we make a deal, ok?" Tía Carmen asked, twisting around to put her hand on my knee.

"I'll stop saying she's gone and you stop saying she's coming back. It's not wrong that we think what we think, Selma, but we only make each other feel worse." And that was the last time either of us spoke about that.

For Mother's Day, Grandma, Tía Carmen, and I had breakfast at a restaurant that served pancakes with a whipped cream swirl so tall it fell over.

"Your mom would be so proud of how you are doing in school," Grandma said.

"I miss her," Tía Carmen said. I had never heard her say it before.

I gave Grandma and Tía Carmen each a card. Grandma cried and Tía Carmen hugged me. I put the one I had for Mom in between the sleeves in our album.

I dreamt with Mom often. Sometimes the dreams were of us on top of a volcano, swimming in lava that tickled our feet and made us laugh. But mostly in my dreams, I searched for her in darkness.

THEN IT'S OVER

Right after the divorce, Dad took my younger brother Manny and me to the barbershop down on Division Avenue. The brick walls were painted a dirty yellow, but some of the white still showed through—the effect was like old teeth piled on top of each other. Though the shop was small, there was room for four metal chairs and a short table with a stack of magazines of different fades. It was the day before my second grade pictures. The barber cut Manny's hair into a tight crop that made his huge eyes look even larger. I stood up, ready to escape, but that's when Dad said, "It's your turn."

"I'm a girl," I said. He smoked his cigarette and ignored me.

At the age of seven, I knew very well not to argue with Dad. If I did, he might lift his shirt to expose his belt, the one with the metal buckle that had left a bruise on my butt the summer before. So, I climbed onto the barber's black chair.

The barber, who had a head of toothpick-sized spikes, covered me with a plastic sheet. It reeked of old men. He squinted at me, and my thick ponytail, and my pink glittery shoes that stuck out underneath the smock. All the other people there were boys and men; all the pictures on the wall were of boys and men. They would probably hang a picture of me, their first ever girl customer, alongside their first dollar bill on the wall.

I saw Dad's reflection in the mirror, saw him nod and Manny stare as my hair fell. I was only supposed to get a trim. But the barber kept cutting. When the scissors finally rested, I started to cry. When I stepped down from the seat and saw the piles of black shiny hair scattered around me, I cried harder. Even when Dad threatened to take off his belt and hit me if I didn't stop crying, I still cried.

"What cute boys," said an old man on our way out.

They didn't put my picture up after all.

When Dad dropped us off, Mom stuck her head through that front window of our house and shouted, "Anna! What happened to your hair?"

I started to cry again and ran to her, collapsing into her arms, as she rubbed my back. Mom bent down and whispered in my ear, "Anna, you are beautiful. Go to your room."

From my room, I heard, "You said to get her a haircut."

"You knew what I meant, Michael!" I closed the door behind me, but I could still hear them fighting.

"You finally let me make a decision and now you are going to bitch about it? If it was so important to you, Jess, why didn't you take her yourself? Too busy being with Nick? Me taking Anna for a haircut isn't about you. Not everything is about you."

"Asshole. I'm not the one displaying my whore around."

"Oh, no. You were much more discreet there for awhile, weren't you, Jess? Just remember. I wasn't the one who stepped out on this marriage first."

The front door slammed and then there was silence. Back when we all lived together, Mom and Dad never really talked except to talk about Manny and me. Most of the time they sent us to our rooms, so they could yell and slam doors.

Now, Manny and I slept in the only bedroom

in the small apartment. We had bunk beds and Mom slept on the sofa bed. Manny cried a lot at night, though, so Mom ended up squeezing in the top bunk with him most nights.

"Give me a couple," I told Manny, and he handed me some curly fries. We'd stopped for burgers at a drive-thru on my way home. At the window, the woman in the paper hat asked Dad what kind of toys we wanted for the kids' meals and I yelled, "One girl!" just in case she thought I was a boy.

I held a curly fry in each hand and lifted them up by my ears so there was one on either side of my head. They looked like pigtails. They also looked nothing like my hair, which had been straight and dark and long.

I popped the fries in my mouth. I didn't know who Nick was, and I was more than mad at Dad, but he had a point. Why didn't Mom take me herself?

"Manny, c'mon. Help me make a wig out of Play-Doh."

Mom woke me up early the next day. She had my plaid dress with the white collar waiting for me. "C'mon, baby," Mom said, coaxing the barrettes shaped like zebras, bows, and bananas into my short hair. She pressed them hard into my scalp, but they didn't hold. She tried a headband next, but it only made my hair stick up. Nothing she tried made me look any better.

"Mom, who's Nick?"

She took a deep breath, but then Dad honked from the driveway. "You guys hurry, now." She jumped up and rushed us to the door. "Manny, don't forget to straighten your tie before they take the picture. And Anna, you have a beautiful face, baby." We put on our hoodie sweaters. Our lunchboxes clanked against the door as it shut behind us.

Dad didn't even look at me as we walked from the house. I yanked open the big heavy door of his old Buick and Manny, in his dark blue dress pants that dragged at the bottom, climbed into the backseat first. I made sure to slam the door hard, but Dad didn't seem to notice. None of us spoke to one another, and although the day was warm for mid-October, I pulled my hood over my head as far as it could go.

When we got to school, Ms. Beatrice told me to remove my hood.

I just shook my head.

"Anna," she said, and I started to tear up. Behind us, all the kids were on the school steps comparing shiny dresses and ties.

"Please, Ms. Beatrice," I whispered, but she made me remove it anyway. Her jaw dropped.

"Anna dear," she said as the wind blew her own long yellow hair into her face. "Sweetie, you can't wear a hood. School rules." She patted me on the back and gently pushed me toward the stairs. "And Anna, if any kids say anything not nice, you tell me."

I nodded. We both knew I wouldn't.

Maggie was waiting at the top of the stairs. Her red dress was peeking from underneath her jean jacket, which was covered in glittery stars. Her hair was hanging free around her face. She smiled at me at first, and then she looked confused.

"What happened?"

I told her everything without crying.

"Here," she said and took off her earrings. They were long, with dangling moons and stars.

"I can't," I said. I didn't have my ears pierced.

"Clip-ons," she said, and pinched them to my ear lobes. "Pretty. Now, c'mon." She grabbed my hand and we walked to class together.

The kids started to laugh as soon as we took our seats. Maggie told them all to be quiet and took her seat at the front of the room. My desk was all the way in the back, but it didn't stop the kids from turning around, sneaking looks over their shoulders as I trudged back alone.

"What's wrong with your hair?" Stevie said.

"What's wrong with your face?" I said back.

Stevie turned around. Maggie gave me a thumbs-up. I sulked into my chair.

The photographer made us all line up in front of the chalkboard. I had to kneel down in front because I was so short. Front and center, so everyone could see my short hair. Behind me, I heard Maggie and some other girls giggling. At least my beat-up shoes were hidden. The kids were used to me not having any new clothes, or new Trapper Keepers, or those fancy juice boxes that weren't really boxes at all. They almost expected me to get a bad haircut, too.

Jane was told to kneel next to me.

"Why did you want your hair so short?" she said.

"I didn't."

"Then where is it?"

"I don't know."

"You look like my cousin José."

"You look like my cousin Hugo."

Jane crossed her arms and grunted.

"Smile," the photographer said.

A flash and it was over.

The Buick was idling in the school parking lot when the bell rang. Manny was already waiting for me outside.

"How was your day?" I asked him.

Manny shrugged his shoulders. We climbed into the Buick and Dad met my eyes this time. He took us to get burgers and fries. Manny and I sat next to each other in the booth, and Dad sat across from us.

"I want you kids to know I tried," Dad said. "I know you love your mom. But I need you to know I really tried to keep us together. Your mom, she just . . . I didn't give up first. Just remember that."

Manny and I kept eating.

In the parking lot, Dad said, "Your grandma had short hair just like you, Anna. She was a beautiful woman." He sighed and pulled out of the lot. "Hair's something that actually comes back."

That night, I ran the hot water in the sink and watched the steam rise in the mirror and before my reflection completely disappeared, I thought I didn't look that bad. Okay, even.

MYRNA'S DAD

My younger cousin Myrna came out of the womb asking questions. *Why does a dog bark? Why is the sun hot? Where is my daddy?*

I was four years older than her, so I could tell her why dogs barked or why the sun was hot, but I had no answer to where her dad was. My Tía Concha never spoke about him.

Once while my Tía Concha was driving us to church, a five-year-old Myrna muttered, "Mommy, where's Daddy?"

From the backseat I could see one of Tía Concha's hands grip the wheel tighter, and the big old car jerked a little.

"He's a clown with the Venezuelan circus. Hey, how about some ice cream before mass?"

This was the first I heard there was an actual clown in the family. I guess it made sense since we never saw him. Myrna giggled, clapped her hands then said she wanted vanilla.

After that, Myrna started telling everyone that her dad was a clown. She'd hit herself on the nose and make a high-pitched sound. She even asked for big red shoes for Christmas. She had super curly hair that looked like our neighbor's poodle, and both her front teeth had fallen out. She'd skip around in a rainbow wig that was so big it dwarfed her face. The *plop-plop* of Myrna's oversized plastic shoes drove my Tía Concha crazy. I could tell by the way her shoulders scrunched up like she was about to sneeze, but she never did tell Myrna to take them off.

At seven, when Myrna and Tía Concha moved in with my parents and me into our tiny Chicago apartment, she walked up to my dad, who was very focused on his lunch, and said, "Tío Ernesto. Do you know where my daddy is?" As he choked on his tostada, my mom said, "Myrna, want Sonia's doll?" and they gave her my favorite doll that cried, drank milk, and burped.

I found this out later when Tía Concha and I got home from the market. I went to my room and there on my bed, on my pillow, was *nothing*.

"Mama, where's Gertrude?" I asked, entering the kitchen where she was at the sink washing dishes.

"I gave it to Myrna. You're much too old for

dolls, mija," she said, not looking at me. "Go do your homework."

Later, I heard Myrna ask again about her dad. This time, Tía Concha said, "No, he's not with the circus anymore. Now, he's an astronaut with the Venezuelan version of NASA. They don't have good phone reception up in space."

"What?" I said. I had never heard about Venezuelans in space. In science class we were learning about the different countries that had space programs and Venezuela was not on the list. I started to ask about it but Mom coughed and when our eyes met, she gave me the look where her eyes narrowed and her lips pursed. It was the look she gave Dad when he had one too many drinks with the compadres. I decided to keep quiet.

That night and for a few weeks following, Myrna drew pictures of jagged stars and crooked planets on paper, on napkins, and one time on my forehead with an orange highlighter when I had fallen asleep on the couch. Pluto was right above my left eye. As I scrubbed my forehead hard with a wet towel, I told Myrna there was no way her dad was in space. She started to cry and Mom yanked me into the kitchen.

"Sonia, you don't say anything about her

father, you understand? You let poor Myrna have her dreams." Then she told me never to bring it up again and sent me to my room.

When Myrna was nine, I caught her crying in the hallway in front of her classroom as my eighth grade class made our way to the gym.

"What's wrong?"

She thrust a flier at me. *Daddy/Daughter Dance* was printed at the top in some fancy, curly font.

"All the other girls' dads are going," she cried.

"When we get home, we'll ask your mom to tell us where your dad is now, ok?"

She nodded and sniffed.

That night at dinner as we all ate frijoles, I took the flier out of my pocket and opened it.

"Tía Concha," I said as she finished slathering sour cream on her plate. "Myrna wants to go to this, so can you tell her where her dad is please?" Everyone stared at the flier.

"Sonia!" Mom cried, slamming her glass down and making the table shake. My dad dropped his fork, which hit the plate with a thump. Tía Concha exhaled so loudly I thought everything on the table was going to blow away, and Myrna's frown was so low, I thought her face was going to droop into the arroz con gandules.

"It's ok," Tía Concha said, putting down her fork. "It's time you know the truth, Myrna."

Myrna and I leaned in, so we could hear every word.

"You're going to tell her *everything*?" Mom's eyebrows jumped toward her scalp.

"Concha, do you really think this story is one for kids to hear?" Dad asked.

"Myrna deserves to finally, really know."

Myrna's dad was neither a Venezuelan clown nor a Venezuelan astronaut. He was a Venezuelan undercover agent. For the past nine years, almost all of Myrna's life, he'd been disguised as a coca plant in the Amazon rainforest, trying to catch drug smugglers. He couldn't contact anyone for fear of putting his family in danger.

When my Tía Concha was finished, my parents both shook their heads. Myrna's face was like a spotlight, bright and round.

"Wow, my dad is cool," Myrna said before going to bed that night.

"That is cool," I said. The coolest job my dad ever had was filling vending machines. Sometimes he'd come home with expired Cheetos or M&Ms.

That night, I thought about Myrna's dad

hiding in the jungle, covered in green and brown paint to make him look like a plant. It didn't make sense. Why wasn't he able to send word home that he was all right? Had he really been on assignment for nine years? Even in the FBI shows I watched on TV, the characters never seemed to be gone for that long. It didn't make sense. I figured next time it came up, I would ask.

A few months later, we all moved to a building over on Cicero Avenue where Tía Concha and Myrna had their own place on the first floor. My parents and I lived on the second. My grandma, who wanted to be near her two daughters and grandkids, moved into the basement.

Our new school was only two blocks away, next to a used car lot. There was a sign with a rabbit driving a Corvette, which made no sense because there were never any rabbits or Corvettes in the lot. Grandma started walking us to and from school. She usually gave Myrna and me a couple of bucks from the slim stack she kept folded in her bra so we could buy cookies that our parents didn't want us to have from the lunchroom.

Once after school, I saw this tall, tan guy with

curly hair wearing pants that were too short at the used car lot. He stood on the porch of the office, which was the size of a port-a-potty, holding a weathered sign that read *Making your dreams come true for only $500 down*. He smoked like he was trying to look cool, like one of those guys with black glossy hair and a matching mustache in the black and white movies Mom liked to watch. He was staring at Myrna as we walked past with our matching book bags and gym shoes—the dark-skinned old ladies at the flea market gave our moms a discount if they bought two or more of the same item. Myrna didn't notice, and we just kept walking.

One afternoon, I asked, "Grandma, why is that man looking at us?" He stood between two rows of beat-up rides, leaning against a station wagon with rusty wheel wells. He took a long drag of his cigarette and kept his eyes on Myrna.

Grandma turned and saw the man, then grabbed me by the wrist and yanked me forward. "Aye, Dios!" She rolled her eyes. "Home. Now."

"But—"

She hushed me. Myrna was too busy singing to herself to notice anything.

When I was supposed to be asleep that night, I heard the adults talking in the kitchen. I tiptoed to my bedroom door and put my ear up to it.

"I need you to hold these for me. Just for a bit. I don't want Myrna to start snooping or find them by accident."

"Yes. Give them to me. I can't believe it, Concha. Out of all the neighborhoods," Mom said.

The next morning while Mom was in the shower and Dad had gone off to work, I noticed something sticking out of Mom's purse on the kitchen counter. I normally wouldn't go through Mom's purse, but technically it wasn't all the way in her purse, and I had feeling it was what Tia Concha gave her. I needed to know what secret they were keeping from Myrna.

In between a sheet of plain paper, I found two photographs wrapped in tissue.

The one on top was of Tía Concha. It was a close-up photo of her kissing a man on the cheek. She looked younger, her hair was much longer, and I could clearly see the mole on her face. The picture was gray, as if it had faded. The man wasn't smiling. I couldn't see the slightest hint of his teeth. His hair was curly and his eyes were light, and his nose almost stuck out of the frame.

The other photograph was of the same man

holding a baby in the crook of his arm, like he was holding a sack of potatoes. He wasn't smiling in this one, either. *Yo Amo Venezuela* was written on his t-shirt, the baby covering the *la* with its chubby hand. They were in front of a White Castle drive-through. I held one photograph in each hand as the flashlight leaned on my legs.

The man in the pictures looked like the man at the car lot only with less wrinkles and a smaller belly. He had a long nose and crazy curly hair that looked like Myrna's. Her hair was all over the place and her light eyes were bright green in the middle, the color of crab apples.

Why would Tía Concha want to hide these photos? Was that man really the guy at the car lot? Was the baby really Myrna?

I put the pictures back and got ready for school.

On the way to school, Myrna said she was going to do her geography report on Venezuela so that she could learn about the country where her father was. When we passed the car lot it was closed, but I still felt Grandma was hurrying, more of a waddle at her old age. School went slowly that day as I thought about finding out if that salesman was really Myrna's dad.

Grandma picked us up after school and we went to Chino's Candy Store. As we exited with our lollipops, Pop Rocks and gum, I asked Grandma again, "Why does that guy from the lot look at Myrna every time we pass by?"

I thought she must have swallowed all her Pop Rocks at once because she started coughing really loud. She reached into her purse and handed a five to Myrna, who was too focused on getting to the center of a Tootsie Roll Pop and hadn't heard what I said. "Myrna, go get Grandma some chocolate, and you get more candy. Take your time." Myrna smiled at me as though she had won something and went inside.

"*Ay! Ay! Ay!*" Grandma cried, and put both her hands on my shoulders. "You ask too many questions! He is no one."

"Grandma, I saw the pictures."

Her mouth gaped then she puffed out her cheeks and exhaled. "Look, your ma and Tía Concha are going to be mad. I'm telling you this because you're old enough now. What are you, sixteen?"

"Thirteen."

"Same thing. That car guy is Myrna's dad."

"Tía Concha said he was an agent in Venezuela."

"Ay, that is bullshit!" I had only heard Grandma swear once before, when her Avon order didn't arrive.

"That's her dad. He ain't no Venezuelan agent. He a Venezuelan *asshole*."

Myrna came out of the store, her lips red from the rope of licorice in her mouth. Grandma lowered her voice as Myrna strolled over to us. "Don't tell Myrna. Her dad never wanted her. Your Tía Concha was the other woman."

Tía Concha was "the other woman?" I had seen the other woman in novellas and they all seemed so evil, with their drawn-on eyebrows, and their massive boobs pushing out of their shrunken fruit-colored dresses, and their big hair. Tía Concha wasn't like that. Why would she be with someone like him? You know, someone *married*?

Myrna handed me some blue cotton candy on a stick and handed a pack of Rollos to Grandma, who stuffed them in her purse. The day was very sunny and the cotton candy began to make my fingers sticky. We were coming up on the car lot. Grandma shot me a look and shook her head.

"Grandma, do you know what Stephanie did in school today?" Myrna began telling her a story that involved vomit and gym shoes, but I stopped paying attention. Instead, I watched the pigeons as they hopped in front of us from place to place, eating crumbs off the sidewalk.

Then I saw him, the salesman, leaning against a yellow van with dark windows. He wore sunglasses and a cream-colored suit with what looked like food stains down the front.

Grandma saw him too and started hurrying again. She was so focused on getting past the lot that neither her nor Myrna, who kept on talking, noticed that I lagged behind. I stopped right in front of him, his feet on the dark asphalt of the parking lot, mine of the light gray of the sidewalk, and stared up. He was tall. I could see his nose was full of long hairs. I noticed a dull yellow ring on his left hand.

"Hey, I know," I said, and he glanced down at me. His face twitched.

"What do you know, huh? That you're annoying me, brat?" His voice was dry and rough.

"Only my dad gets to call me a brat," I said. I stood very still and straight, like I was supposed to do in church. "I know you're Myrna's dad."

"You know nothing," he said. He dropped his cigarette on the ground and stepped on it. His hand shook as he put it in his pocket. Maybe because I saw one too many movies where people knew stuff they shouldn't, I stared up those nostrils, at his quivering lip, at his enormous hazel eyes, and said, "Does your old lady know?" I said "old lady" like I'd heard it on TV.

"Hijole!" Grandma yelled. She pulled at my arm.

"What's wrong, Grandma?" Myrna asked.

Grandma just snarled at Myrna's dad. He blinked and hurried away.

"Wait 'til I talk to your parents," Grandma said to me, and pinched my arm. She was breathing heavily. Myrna kept asking what I had said to the man. I gazed at her. She looked so much like him.

"Nothing," I said. "You can have the rest of my candy."

That night while Myrna slept, my parents sat me down in the kitchen.

"So, you know what we know," Mom began. She blew into the mug she held. Steam from the tea rose into the air.

"Now, listen. You should get in trouble for going through your mom's things and for talking to that man, but you won't because you aren't going to tell Myrna. Understand?" Dad said.

"Yes, I get it."

"This whole thing with Concha and Pedro should've never happened in the first place," Dad said, and then sent me to my room.

The next day after school, Grandma held my wrist the whole way home. When we passed the lot, the man was nowhere to be found. He was replaced with a short white man with hair as yellow as lemon drops. I never did see Myrna's dad again.

At thirteen, Myrna asked her mom about her dad again.

"I haven't heard from him, mija, and I probably never will," Tía Concha said. "He's gone for good. I don't want to ever talk about this again."

Myrna cried for weeks. Sometimes she'd cry alone in her room, but most times she cried in mine, sprawled out on my bed as I rubbed her back, or sitting at my desk, staring out the window as I pushed away the hair that stuck to her wet face.

My Tía Concha told me once that she was grateful I kept what I knew a secret.

"I'm rather embarrassed by it all. I don't want her to think bad about me. I love Myrna very much, and all he wanted was for me to get rid of her. That's what he said, 'Get rid of it.' Every time I reached out to him, he called Myrna the worse things. He only saw her one time when

she was a baby because I begged him. Then he
told me to leave him alone. I thought it was better to make her think he wanted her than to tell
her that he couldn't care less about her. I know
how that feels."

On the day when Myrna turned eighteen, she
and I were lounging in the backyard. The sun
was hot on our skin.

"Sonia, do you know anything about my dad?"

I thought of telling her we should go get ice
cream or offer her those earrings of mine I knew
she really liked. I thought of all the times her
mother didn't tell her the truth. All the times my
silence was like a lie.

Her eyes didn't leave mine, and staring at
her face, I was reminded how much she looked
like him.

I decided to tell her everything.

THE KEYS

I was thirteen the summer I went to El Salvador to visit my abuelos. They had just moved there from the States. They lived off the busiest street in Cojutepeque, not entirely the poorest in the city. Near their house there was a six-corner intersection of three unpaved streets with no stop signs. I never saw an accident while I was there, but one time I found a dead dog in the ditch, and another time, a dead horse sprawled out on the edge of the road. The careless drivers were long gone.

After a week, I got to know my abuelos pretty well. Abuela went to church every morning at 8:00 am and stayed there 'til 9:30, went to the cemetery to visit her mother, taught English for free to whoever wanted to learn in the park, stopped by the panadería to get pastries for her afternoon coffee, spoke with the street vendors who sold Levi jeans, and returned home around noon.

I went with her the first few days, but I was

too tired to listen to the priest speak Spanish way too fast for me to comprehend. Afterward, Abuela introduced me to everyone, and they all asked me about Chicago and how much money my parents made. After that, Abuela said I could sleep in as long as I prayed the rosary with her at night.

Abuelo waited 'til I woke up around 10:00 am to take me to the mercado so I could buy souvenirs I didn't need: scrunchies that didn't hold my hair, t-shirts with GUANACA spelled out across the front, and a taxidermy lizard smoking a cigarette in one claw and holding a miniature Salvadorean flag in the other. Sometimes we went for a stroll around the neighborhood, where people on the sidewalks with colorful cloth bags and sombreros moved slowly against the river of yellow and red scooters that zipped down the dirt roads.

Back in the States, Abuelo took me to the circus and the movies. He told me stories about how, when he was a kid, no one thought he spoke Spanish because he was part British. Before they moved, he showed me how to punch someone in the stomach hard enough to knock the wind out them, just in case any boys tried to make a move.

After a week, our routine changed. We didn't

go for a walk or to the mercado. Instead, we went to a new neighborhood.

"Don't tell Abuela, ok, Sara? She doesn't like Fernando," he said as we entered a small concrete house painted the color of pistachios. Inside, Abuelo drank tequila and played poker with Don Fernando, whose kids I taught to say "Hello, I need to pee," in English.

I covered for him that night when Abuela asked him why he smelled like fried chicken, which he wasn't supposed to eat because of his high cholesterol.

"I didn't have any fried chicken. I know how bad it is for my heart," Abuelo said.

"I ate the fried chicken, Abuela," I blurted out, even though I hated fried chicken.

"Try to eat better, Sara, ok?" she said, and smiled at us both. When she looked away, Abuelo grinned at me.

A few days after that Abuelo started acting strange. From my bed, I'd hear him get up in the mornings right after Abuela left for church. I heard him turn on the shower in the bathroom. The floorboards creaked as he walked around in his room and made his way out the front door.

I didn't think anything of it at first, but it kept happening. When I asked him where he

went, Abuelo would only shake his head. I had
to know. One morning, I didn't go back to sleep
after he left. Instead, I watched him through
my bedroom window. Through the dust on the
glass, I saw Abuelo go not in the direction of Don
Fernando's, or in the direction of the mercado, or
even to the chicken joint. He took a street I had
never seen him take before. I watched for as long
as I could before he disappeared.

Later that day, he got home right before
Abuela, breathing heavy and giving me a thumbs
up, as though he'd won a race. He went straight
to the bathroom and by the time he got out,
Abuela had arrived, pouring coffee and putting
the pasteles on the kitchen table. I began cutting
queso fresco into little triangles so we could have
them with the tortillas.

"You two stayed in this morning?" Abuela
asked as she stirred the frijoles and warmed the
tortillas right over the open flames on the stove.
She never burned her hands, just flipped the tortillas without really even looking, until the ends
curled and the center bore small dark spots.

"Sara and I took it easy," he said, winking so
only I could see.

"Yup," I lied, and hoped that Abuela didn't
hear me when I swallowed hard.

It was 8:00 pm that night, the universal time that all old people in El Salvador fall asleep, including my abuelos. I said goodnight to them both. Abuela began snoring almost immediately. My plan was to stay up 'til Abuelo took his nightly trip to the fridge and then make him tell me where he had *really* been going. While I waited, I took a long, cool shower and then watched some reruns of *Cops* and the ending of *The Terminator*, which was on the only English-speaking channel their cable picked up. I understood Spanish completely, I just didn't like Spanish television shows.

After two hours, the cable went out—again. I didn't think Abuelo would mind if I woke him up to fix it. This American girl needed her TV! I tiptoed into their room. But Abuela was alone in the bed in her ivory nightgown.

Shocked, I moved away and banged my knee into the steel frame of the bed. Abuela stirred awake.

"Everything ok?" she slurred.

"Yes, Abuela."

She turned onto her back and felt the empty side beside her. "Where's your abuelo?" she muttered.

Maybe he had gone back to Don Fernando's for another game, or to the chicken joint, or to the mystery place he went in the mornings. Wherever he was, he went without telling Abuela and I didn't know if I should be the one to point out that he wasn't in the house.

"The cable. It went out. I asked Abuelo to fix it, so that's what he's doing. Fixing it. Go back to sleep, Abuela," I said, and kissed her forehead. She turned to her other side this time, and by the time I tiptoed out of the room, she was snoring again.

Abuelo must have gone out when I was in the shower and thought I wouldn't come looking for him. He never went out at night though; Abuela was too paranoid that something would happen to him. "This neighborhood is very different after dark. That's why we stay inside when night comes," she had said.

I wanted to stay up so I could make Abuelo tell me where he had gone. But I ended up falling asleep on the couch. I woke up to Abuelo telling Abuela that he'd had a good night's sleep.

"I know you went somewhere," I whispered later, when Abuela was out of the room.

"Sara, you must have been dreaming," he replied, and then Abuela came back into the room and I didn't say anything more.

That night, I pretended to go to sleep early. I faked a yawn loud enough for my abuelos to hear and then didn't move in bed. A little later, I heard Abuela snoring, and sometime after that, from the sound of the floors creaking, I knew Abuelo was up. When I heard the click of the front door closing, I went to the window. On the dark street below me, I saw Abuelo's tall shadow hurrying down the same strange street.

I took the stairs up to the roof. I would have a clear view from there, so when he came back, I would be ready to stand in the hallway with my arms crossed and make him tell me what was going on.

The house had only two stories, but the air on the roof was cool. The wind blew my hair gently and I shivered. I could taste El Salvador on my lips. The roofs surrounding me were painted different colors. It made the neighborhood look like a game board.

Early on in my visit, my abuelos told me that security guards with machine guns marched along the roof of the bank next door at night. I didn't know whether to believe them, since I was really only supposed to be on the roof during the day.

I settled on the ledge and took my eyes off of

the sky long enough to glimpse a hulking silhouette on the roof next to me. Moonlight shined on the gun at his hip and on his bulletproof vest. I saw two other guards on the adjacent side of the building. They had guns, too. One nodded to me and the other never looked my way, but I was sure he knew I was there.

I heard the rumble of loud music and peered across the street. I was like one of those men next to me, silent in the shadows, minus the gun.

The front door of Rosita's Casita across the street opened. The door bore a painting of a naked woman with a moon-shaped face and big breasts. Abuela told me to study hard so I wouldn't grow up to be like the girls that worked there, selling their bodies by dancing for drunk men that had wives.

During the day it was closed. There were rusted metal bars over the windows and the old ladies who sold their mangos and tamales and tortillas camped in front of it. They had long silver braids on either side of their shoulders and dressed in yellows, blues and reds. The younger women had chubby babies wrapped against their bodies. The city felt different than it did during the day, when it was a chaos of horns, screeching brakes and vendors shouting about what they were selling. "¡Tortillas! ¡Elotes! ¡Pupusas!"

One of the times I did go to church with Abuela, another parishioner made a face like she smelled something bad and pointed to a woman sitting a few pews over.

The old parishioner said, "How can she show up here?"

The woman she pointed to was maybe in her fifties. Her hair was pulled back in a tight bun, and a large pink birthmark spread across one of her cheeks like a country on a map. Her sweater was buttoned to the top, despite the stuffy heat inside the church. She clapped her hands when the priest said something that made everyone roar.

When I asked about the woman later, Abuela only said, "Rosita should be ashamed of herself." Not too long after that, I figured out that Rosita owned the club with the naked woman on the door.

As I stood on the roof, I glared down at Rosita's. In the glow from the streetlamp, I could see an older man in khaki pants with a woman with a long ponytail that hit the middle of her back. I watched as the man slid his hand down into her short skirt.

On the roof of the bank, the security men were still patrolling, oblivious or just plain ignoring the couple across the street. The old man and the young woman didn't look like bank robbers, so I guess they didn't call for any special attention. The guards weren't paying attention to me either, so even though I knew I should have turned away, I continued to watch the couple.

The man was touching her and hugging her. He leaned into her, saying something that I couldn't hear. She cackled and hit him on his chest, said something back. This happened a few times until he shoved his hand further down her skirt. She rubbed her thumb and fingers together right in front of his face. He reached way down into the pockets of his pants and pulled out some bills, and waved them in her face. That's when I saw Abuelo come around the corner with a woman I had never seen before.

He walked down the street toward the house with his hands in the pockets of the clean, crisp pants Abuela ironed for him. The woman had long, bright red hair the color of ketchup. They didn't touch as they strolled past the corner store that sold calling cards and Jarritos, past the panaderia that sold bread filled with coconut and pudding and cheese.

When they reached Rosita's, Abuelo opened the door. He and the woman walked right in.

I looked around, wondering if someone else had seen it.

"Hey," I said, trying to catch the attention of the guard nearest me. "Did you see that guy?" I don't know what I expected the guard to say. He studied me for a few moments, and then I realized he didn't speak English.

I threw my hands up in frustration. I shooed the guard away and he turned back to begin his patrol once more.

I knew what happened in places like that. At my school in the States, this group of seventh grade boys had been caught with magazines of naked women, but not before they had showed everyone in class. I had felt bad for the women in the photos.

I decided I had to go in there and get Abuelo out. I'd grab Abuela's key she usually kept near the door, make my way across the street and bring Abuelo home before Abuela woke up. But when I went downstairs to grab it, the hooks that held Abuela's and Abuelo's keys were both empty.

At breakfast the next morning, I watched Abuela take her pills with a glass of water. She had aged more than Abuelo, it seemed. She walked on her own, but slowly. She complained often of the aches in her bones. The last time she needed help carrying groceries, I was shocked at her lack of strength, at the fragility of her arms.

On the table between us was Abuela's small coin purse and it was opened. There peeking out, in the middle of all the change, was her key attached to a keychain of a miniature wooden cross. I watched Abuela hang it back up on the hook right next to Abuelo's key. "This way I will remember where I put it," she said.

"You look tired, Sara," Abuelo said at dinner.

"You do, too," I said, and then excused myself, saying I needed to get more rest.

I wished that Abuelo would stay home, or that Abuela would decide to pull an all-nighter praying or making tortillas so he wouldn't have a chance to leave. But nothing like that happened.

I knew he wouldn't tell me the truth if I asked, so I waited for Abuela's snoring and his footsteps, and front door closing before I went downstairs. I checked the hooks. This time, the key Abuela had hung up earlier was there. I snatched her key. Both hooks empty now.

I rubbed the wooden cross keychain between

my sweaty fingers. Abuelo was just entering the club wearing the white shirt I had brought for him as a gift from back home. It had CHICAGO printed in bold black letters across his back. Had he turned around, he would have seen me there in front of the house in my monkey pajama pants. But he went inside.

The street was empty except for a dog sniffing at the curb and the red light flashing above the door to Rosita's. I crossed the street and hopped over a pile of garbage at the curb. I stopped in front of the door to Rosita's. The naked woman seemed to be moving under the flickering light blub. Then the door opened, and out came the woman I had seen with Abuelo the night before. From this close, I saw her eyes were dull underneath the thick purple eye shadow she wore, and her hair was pulled back so tight it looked like it hurt.

"You shouldn't be here, kid," she said in Spanish. Then she turned toward a whistle that was coming from a man down the block. I watched her strut into the shadows before opening the door and going inside.

I caught a glimpse of a group of naked women dancing on a stage beneath the flash of strobe lights. I took a step forward, but was immediately blocked by an enormous man with a white shirt whose buttons struggled to stay together. His hair was gray and coarse like a Brillo pad.

"What are you doing here?" he said in Spanish.

"My abuelo is in there," I said, flustered. I pointed inside.

The man managed to turn just his thick neck to the side and yelled, "Hey, someone's grand-daughter is here."

"A lot of granddaughters are here," someone answered, and laughter erupted at the bar.

"Chicago," I said, and pointed to my shirt. The enormous man nodded this time. He turned around and said, "You!" When he moved to the side, Abuelo was there.

Abuelo stood up, rushed over to me and grabbed me by the wrist. He pulled me out of the club. Sweat covered his forehead and his mus-tache drooped. His hand shook as we crossed the street to go back to the house. I jogged to keep up with him.

"Why?" I asked as he tried to open the front door, but his hand was quivering so much he couldn't get his key in the lock.

I pushed him aside and pushed the key I had into the keyhole, but I didn't turn it. The wooden cross keychain swung back and forth.

"Tell me now," I said, and started to cry.

"I'm sorry, Sara. I'm sorry." His voice trembled and he wiped my eyes.

"What if Abuela wakes up?"

"I will tell her where I was. You don't need to cover for me anymore."

"I don't understand why you went there."

"Neither do I, but I'll never go back. I promise you. I didn't mean to hurt you or your abuela," he said. He turned the key in the door, and we stepped inside. We could hear Abuela snoring upstairs.

The next morning, Abuela went to church and Abuelo took me to the mercado. We didn't talk about what happened. He bought me a strawberry-filled churro and Abuela a new sweater. That night all three of us watched *The Terminator*. Abuela fell asleep halfway through with her head on Abuelo's shoulder.

The rest of my summer there, Abuelo never snuck out in the mornings or at night again.

Both keys stayed side by side on the hooks.

ON THE WAY

People used to say I was my daddy's girl. I went everywhere with him, to the store, to the mechanic, to his poker games because he said I was his good luck charm. He and Mom would laugh when they weren't fighting. Things never seemed that bad, but when Dad left for work one day and didn't come home, I didn't know why.

"He's just gone, baby," Mom had said. Soon after that, she began working double shifts, and Grandma—Dad's mom, moved in with us a little after that. She'd been kicked out of her nursing home for cursing out the staff and throwing things at the other patients. Again.

Mom wouldn't tell me where Dad went, and after a few weeks I stopped asking. But I wrote him letters that I crammed into blank envelopes and put in the mailbox down the street. I never told anyone about this, not even my best friend,

Benny. I knew they would never get to Dad, but they had to go somewhere, I figured.

Grandma yanked me by the arm, her nails, chewed jagged while waiting for the Cicero bus, dug into my skin. The bus doors opened and she pulled me up the steps, as though afraid I would try to escape.

"She nine," Grandma yelled at the bus driver, a fat woman with CTA stretched beyond recognition on her wide blue sleeve. The bus driver bent at the waist as far as she could. One of her hairy brows raised and she eyed me up and down like I was a criminal.

"You nine?" she asked me. I felt Grandma's nails on the back of my neck and I nodded.

"She nine," Grandma said again. Sighs and a couple of *c'mons* echoed from the back. I hadn't been nine for five years.

The bus driver waved her big hand and we boarded. There were two empty seats left— one way in the back where some kids sat and laughed, and one toward the front where the old people were. Grandma said nothing and shoved me into the seat between two old folks that reeked of Bengay and hairspray.

"You're not nine," said one of the old ladies.

Her hands were shaking, and the bunch of keys that hung off the strap of her purse jangled. Her lips were thin and wrinkled, just like the rest of her. She had big brown blotches on her face, the color of the oatmeal cookies we ate at home.

"Yeah, you're not nine," said the other. Her lips had no wrinkles, but her hands had big blue veins, like pipes beneath her skin.

I did what I usually do when I don't know what to say to strangers. I acted like I didn't understand.

I shook my head and raised my arms, my palms toward the sky like I was balancing an invisible glass in each one. It was easier than explaining Grandma didn't want to dish out an extra buck to let me on the bus even though she had wads of cash in her bra. I had watched her take out a stack of bills, damp with sweat and smelling like the Walgreen's perfume she wore, to pay for things like vitamins and pantyhose at stores.

The old lady with permed hair shook her head. She sneered at me and said, "You're a liar. You should be ashamed of yourself."

Her words made my skin itch. I looked to my side and the other old lady was nodding in agreement. I leaned even further to scan the back of the bus, past the couple making out, and the baby crying and flailing its arms like it was winding up to fly away, and spotted Grandma eating one of her cookies that she always kept inside her purse, wrapped in, like, twenty napkins. I wanted to get up, walk over, and yank that cookie out of her mouth. She'd put me in that seat. She'd refused to pay because she was cheap. She dragged me everywhere since Mom had to go to work. And she was the one that made sure I knew that my dad left almost half a year ago because Mom and I didn't make him happy. I stared at Grandma and wished she could feel my eyes on her.

In the mornings, she'd stomp from our spare room and plop down at the breakfast table. It was my responsibility to make sure we ate since Mom had to leave for work before the sun came up. Grandma would shoot herself up with the medicine for her diabetes and wait at the table 'til I was finished cooking breakfast: eggs, no salt, toast, no butter, hand-squeezed orange juice from the oranges she got from the guy that sold fruit out of the back of his truck.

We got mangos from the fruit truck guy, too. I loved mangos. I loved slicing them up in three perfect pieces and sprinkling them with chili powder and lemon juice and sucking the juice from them. Dad taught me how to eat mangos like that. We'd sit on the back porch and he would scrunch up his face and smile, "This chili is hot. Too hot for you, Lucia." I would take him up on his challenge. I would take a piece of mango off his plate, the fruit slimy under my fingertips, raise it to my lips, the juices dripping onto my lap, and take a bite. I'd try not to make a face, but he would watch me and laugh when my eyes began watering.

I was staring at the floor of the bus when I saw Grandma's familiar shoes. "Vamanos," she said, and hurled me off my seat. I turned back to the two old ladies, but neither of them bothered to look at me.

She wouldn't let go of my wrist as we walked. This meant she was tired, and with her swollen ankles, couldn't walk as fast as I could. She used me to keep her balance.

In these moments, moments when she needed me—like when she couldn't get the needle in, or needed me to make her breakfast—she didn't say one word about Mom. Didn't call her bad words in Spanish and say she was the reason my father left because "a real wife stayed home and didn't go out to work," the reason I was a spoiled brat, the reason she was going to die without seeing her son again because we drove him away. Mom told me Grandma was just old and bitter and to ignore her, but all I wanted to do was yell at her. I think Mom hoped that Dad would come back one day and see how great she was for taking care of *his* mother.

"Alli," she said pointing to some dirty, stone building that looked abandoned.

"What is this place?" I said, but Grandma, who understood more English than she let on, just slapped me on the back and pushed me toward the door.

The lobby smelled musty. A dusty gumball machine with no gumballs sat in the corner. Almost all the seats in the room were filled with women; the only males were babies, cradled in their mothers' laps. One little boy with barely any hair played alone near a chair with a teensy paper cup.

Grandma approached the counter and said she had an appointment. Behind it a woman took down her name. They spoke in Spanish. I didn't let Grandma know that I knew more Spanish than I let on. The lady told us to take a seat. We sat together next to a woman who anxiously tapped her feet, like she was sending

Morse code. From a bottle with a picture of a strawberry on it, she rubbed pink lotion into the folds of fat in her arms. The too-sweet smell of it filled the lobby.

"Fabian!" a nurse yelled from an open door by the counter just a few minutes later. We both stood. Grandma pushed me on the back of my head to move me forward.

The nurse showed us to a room at the end of a narrow hallway. A man with a white coat stood there holding a clipboard. He smirked at me and I immediately didn't like him.

"Hola, Doña Miriam," he said, and they kissed on the cheek like they were old friends. "Is this little Lucia?" he said in English.

"Humph. Not so little," Grandma said in Spanish. She grabbed my stomach and pinched it. I winced. "She's eats like a boy. She eats everything."

"We can take care of that," the man said, and then looked at me.

He turned and picked up a syringe off the table. "You should lose twenty pounds. How old are you, Lucia?"

"Almost fourteen," I said. I stared at the syringe.

"See? Now is the time. You'll want a boyfriend

soon. Now, lower your pants. I need to give this shot in your behind."

"Ahorita," Grandma said.

"No." I stepped back.

"Lucia, don't be scared. It's just a shot of B12 and lipotropic. It will make you beautiful. I'll give you pills, too."

He got closer and I could see the brown liquid in the syringe. I shook my head. Grandma slapped me hard. I kept my face still, refusing to show it hurt even as the pain shot into my cheekbone and stayed there. The doctor stayed silent.

"Ahorita," Grandma repeated, and I unbuttoned my pants and pulled them down. The needle felt as thick as a tree as it slid beneath my skin and then slowly came back out. I wanted to cry, but held it in.

"Good. Now, maybe I can finally say she's my granddaughter."

I didn't know if my face was hot from the slap still, or if the medicine from the shot was surging through my body, or that it was simply the anger I had that made me feel flushed. I walked into the lobby and surveyed the room. I guess all the women were there for the same reason. They all wanted shots and pills. They all wanted to be pretty. The pain from the shot spread to my chest as we walked out of the building and into the bright sun. Grandma smiled at me for the first time in awhile, as though whatever had been in that shot was transforming me already.

The next morning, Mom was still working her double shift, so I didn't have a chance to tell her. Grandma called me from the kitchen.

"Yes, Grandma," I said. I trudged over to the fridge and took out the eggs and the cheese and the oranges. She sat at the table rubbing alcohol on a cotton ball over the same spot on her thigh, blue veins thin as strands of hair under her skin.

"It's almost six months since your dad left. You know why, don't you?"

The eggs slowly began to cook. I carelessly turned them over in the warming pan. I didn't like to see her inject herself. She always made it a point to make a face that showed how much it pained her.

After she was done, she rubbed the injection with the same cotton ball and said, "He left because you're fat, Lucia. Who wants a fat daughter?" She drank her orange juice. A little spilled from the corner of her mouth. She tapped her plate and I pushed the eggs, brown with cheese, from the skillet. She picked up her fork, and stuck me in the side. "I'd be embarrassed, too. Did you take those pills the doctor gave you?"

I sat down next to her. I didn't need those pills. I didn't want that shot, but I didn't know what to say to her. A bit of egg stuck to the mole near her mouth. I nodded, but we both knew I was lying. I hadn't taken those pills. She hit my hand with her fork, and I got up and went to my room. I heard her humming as I grabbed the pill bottle.

When I came back to the kitchen, there was a glass of water in front of my seat. I opened the bottle and threw a pill into my mouth. It wasn't coated and the sour taste almost made me gag. I took a big gulp of the water and swallowed.

"Now, remember. Don't tell your mother about this. I'm just trying to help. When your dad comes back for me, maybe he'll stay this time. If you and your mother can get it together." She ate the last of her eggs. I waited 'til she was done to wash the dishes, and when I heard her snore from her late afternoon nap, I snuck out of the house in hopes of finding Benny.

Benny used to look up to my dad. He lived down the block in a house with a yard where the bushes were groomed to look like different animals: a dinosaur, a llama, and a spider, even. His dad and mine had been friends long before we were even born. Benny's mom had left years ago, so now it was just him and his dad.

Benny and I liked to go to the park down the street. We'd talk about movies or school, or sometimes we'd talk about his mom and where she could have gone. Sometimes we'd talk about my dad and why he left. We could only wonder because no one ever told us anything.

I found Benny in the park playing basketball by himself. He waved at me and jogged over. My stomach got a nervous feeling, probably from the pill I'd taken. I wanted to tell him what Grandma was making me do. As we started walking, he slung his arm around my shoulder, holding the basketball in the other. Benny said, "Walking with you must be what it's like to get hip checked in the NHL." He laughed and pushed me playfully.

There was no one in the park. Benny was wearing the track jacket that used to be his dad's. The wind blew my hair around and some strands stuck to my lips. Some birds called to one another between the trees and the sun came out, making our shadows darker. I watched mine, falling on the pathway bordered by dying grass, swaying left to right as I walked. My hips nearly took up the whole sidewalk.

"Benny likes you," Julia had told me one day in class. "He's gonna try to kiss you soon and probably feel you up." We giggled. I hoped now that he'd grab me and kiss me. I'd even let him feel me up, even though I didn't really have any boobs.

Benny's shadow came closer to mine, both of them stretched out on the cement like people bigger than us. I looked up at him. Benny's pimples were all in one cluster on his forehead, but everywhere else his skin was smooth like an apple. He smiled at me. He had those clear braces that you could still see.

"You mad?" he said.

"Nope," I said, and he put his arm around me again. Our shadows were one for a moment.

"Seriously, hip check!" He laughed again and we stopped underneath a tree. We were almost in high school, and we would be going to different ones. I knew that soon, things would change for us. New schools. New friends. New girls around him. Who knew if we would still hang out as much?

Nothing ever stayed the same for long. Mom

and Dad proved that. I wanted to tell him how Grandma called me fat, how Mom was always working, how I'd been crying in my room a lot lately. I wanted to tell him this, but I didn't want to lose him, too. I didn't want to drive him away like Dad, so instead I didn't say a word.

Underneath that tree, Benny turned his head one way, then the other, and finally kissed me. I heard the basketball fall to the ground, his hands on my hips. We opened our mouths, our tongues touched, and his soft lips met mine. I got lost in that moment for a while.

"I better get back before my grandma wakes up," I said when it was over, and he smiled.

"Yeah. She's crazy."

When we got to my house, we stopped out front and we smiled again. "Let's meet up tomorrow," Benny said.

"Sure thing." I said and he gave him a peck on the cheek.

When I walked inside my house, my smile disappeared when I saw my Dad sitting on the couch. Grandma sat next to him.

He was wearing the shirt that I had given him a few months back for Fathers Day, right before he left. It was so white against his dark arms. His hair was longer than it had been when he'd left, and wavier than I remembered. His glasses were perched mid-nose like always, and he pushed them up when he saw me. His eyes were wide, the amber speckles in them twinkling like they used to do when he'd tell me he loved me. He stepped forward, his arms rising up slowly, like strings were lifting them. I noticed he wasn't wearing his wedding ring.

"Lucia," he said. Grandma held tight to his hand, not letting it go. "I'm sorry I left the way I did. It's just—"

I didn't let him finish. I ran out of the house and called after Benny, who waited for me to catch up. I pretended not to hear Dad shouting my name.

Benny waved at him. "Hey, your dad is back!" he said, and started to walk back toward my house.

"No!" I took his hand. "Please, Benny." I didn't need to say anymore. He knew from my eyes, my voice, in the way I touched his wrist that I had to go. He held onto my hand and we walked together toward his house.

"Why don't you want to see your dad? I thought you would be happy," Benny said. We sat on his couch. The house was quiet, his father out.

"I don't want to talk about it," I said, but I did. I wanted to tell Benny everything. Instead of words, I began to cry and he put his arm around me again.

"C'mon," he said after a minute. He stood up and grabbed my hand. "You need to go talk to your dad."

"No."

"Lucia, if it were my mom who came back, I would talk to her. You're lucky."

"Fine," I said.

He walked me back to my house.

"I have to be back before my pop gets home, but call me or come over later, ok?"

I nodded and went up the stairs to my front door.

When I wandered into my house, Grandma was still on the couch. Dad sat next to her and looked up from his hands when he heard me come in.

"Lucia. Please, let me explain," he said. I followed him into the kitchen. We stood on opposite sides of the kitchen table.

"Your mom and I, we just got married so young and . . . "

"So you left? You just left without saying anything?"

I started crying, but didn't bother wiping the tears away. I clenched my fists at my sides so tight, my knuckles hurt.

"I know you're mad. I'm sorry. I just couldn't take the fighting between your mom and me anymore. When we both knew there was just no love there. When we finally said it, I just needed to go away and breathe. I shouldn't have left that way, I know. I don't expect you to understand or even forgive me. Just give me another chance. I'll never leave like that again. I love you." He pulled out a kitchen chair and sat down. He put his elbows on the table and cried into his palms.

"Does Mom know you're here?" I didn't want to see him cry, but I had been crying for months too.

He nodded. I crossed my arms, feeling my heart ram into my chest.

"I used the time away to get things in order. I got my own place not too far away from here. I'm taking Grandma to live with me. She and your mom never got along anyway. Do you want to come see it? You can visit anytime you want. Your mom said it's up to you." He wanted me to say yes. I wanted to say yes, too.

"No."

"Lucia, I didn't leave because of you," Dad said as I walked out of the kitchen, not turning back.

I hid under the covers until the house was quiet. I left my room, only hearing my footsteps. I threw the pills into the sink and washed them down the garbage disposal. I pushed the chair Dad had sat in back underneath the table and stepped out onto the back porch. On the step was a plate of mango, cut up in three perfect pieces. A small black bug crawled across the plate. I kicked it away. I wiped my eyes and looked up at the sky. There was no moon, no stars. I waited for Mom to come home.

AT THIS MOMENT

When Grandpa called me to tell me of the news, I could hardly understand him because he was crying so hard. I ached for them both. My grandparents were the only two people I had in my life from my father's side, and now one was gone.

Inside the funeral home, there was a sign with Grandma's name spelled in white letters. Quiet chatter came through the open door of the parlor. A group of small children horsed around in the corner, sucking on lollipops. Some adult tried to hush them with a quick, ineffective *shhhh*.

A wooden coffin sat at the front of the room beneath the glow of a bright light. Bouquets of flowers in vases had been propped on stands all around the coffin. Most of the people in the room sat in the chairs lined up in rows. Some drank coffee from small Styrofoam cups and spoke in hushed voices. From where I stood, I could only see Grandma's head propped up on a pillow.

A large woman I didn't know stopped before me. "My, aren't you Miguel's girl?" she asked. Two old men in black suits to our side turned and peeked at us. "Not that you're a girl anymore. Look at you, all grown." She grabbed my wrist. "I'm sorry about your grandma, honey."

The woman wore bright orange lipstick and her hair was stiff with hairspray. It was styled high and dyed an unnatural black. "Your daddy's right over there. It's nice how he came in from Florida." She pointed to a huge bouquet of red and pink and white roses behind her.

From behind the bouquet appeared a man that I remembered too well. His hair had grayed, but I remembered that walk, the exaggerated sway from side to side. I remember his mouth, too, with its crowded teeth that stuck out so his lips didn't meet when they were closed. This man, who I had not seen in twenty years, was my father.

He didn't come toward me, but stood alone, staring at the coffin. One of his hands was balled into a fist. He had gained weight since I had seen him last. His black jacket bunched around his shoulders. Suddenly, he turned away from the casket. His dark eyes met mine, and he mouthed my name.

I hurried past him to the coffin, searching the room for Grandpa, but I couldn't find him. I knelt before the coffin and put my hand on my grandma's. It was like a doll's. Her skin felt cold, her fingers were stiff. I closed my eyes and whispered, "Please make him go away."

I felt everyone watching me. Kneeling in my long gray coat, I imagined I must have looked like a fallen statue. I stood up and kissed Grandma's forehead. It felt like plastic.

I turned around. I could no longer spot my father. Maybe he left when he saw me. Maybe he was hiding somewhere. I finally saw Grandpa sitting down near the back with his head in his hands. The men sitting with him seemed relieved when I came over, and left us alone.

"Grandpa," I said, and knelt next to him. The rough carpet scraped my tights. I rubbed his back, then slowly pulled his hands away from his face.

He looked at me, but didn't see me. I wiped his eyes with my coat sleeve and when he finally noticed me, he pulled me into his arms. We began to sob.

"Here's your water."

I froze. The voice was empty, emotionless.

I stood up and turned to face my father.

"Hello, mija."

The last big fight my parents had, I snuck out of my room and tiptoed down the short hallway. I slipped underneath my father's desk. It was a small nest of wires that reeked of beer.

"Did you think I didn't know about you and Lovie?" Mom asked.

From beneath the desk, I watched my father's fist smash the glass of the framed picture of me with my grandparents. Blood began to drip from his hand onto the floor.

Then he turned on Mom.

I screamed. They both turned to look at me.

"Elena," they said in unison. I ran upstairs. Some neighbors had called the cops, and I stayed in my room and listened to Mom tell the officers nothing had happened. After that, she told my father to move out and then filed for divorce.

That summer brought my tenth birthday. My father decided it was time for a road trip to Florida, where I would spend a week with him and his new girlfriend, who was already waiting for us in their new home.

"Mija, pass me some more," my father said, holding out his right hand as he drove. I reached into the gigantic box of Goldfish crackers and put a school of them in his hand. A while later, he pulled into a parking lot. We'd been driving all day. He told me to wait in the car while he paid for a room and got a key. The motel had two stories. All the doors to the rooms were the same faded yellow, all the curtains in the window the same shade of brown.

The sun was setting when my father came back to the car. He had lost weight since the divorce. Apparently when he and Lovie moved to Florida, Lovie left all her cooking skills behind. She had been my babysitter for a few months and I guessed one day she'd probably end up being my stepmother.

"Let's go, Elena." He reached into the backseat and grabbed our bags. I followed him, carrying the pillow I had brought from home. The room had washed-out, orange carpeting marked with a trail of teeny cigarette burns. I went to turn on the lamp, but it didn't work. With only one petite ceiling light, the room was dark. I noticed there was only one bed.

"Pop, where you going to sleep?" There wasn't a couch or any other furniture he could sleep on.

"This is all they had. Now, go change into your pajamas. We've got to get an early start tomorrow."

I went into the bathroom and tried not to touch anything because the sink had a brown circle of sludge in it and there was a dead fly near the door.

"C'mon. What are you doing in there?" Pop yelled. He sounded angry.

I opened the bathroom door. Pop was already in bed under the covers on one side of the bed. I went on the other side and sat on top of the blankets.

"Why are you acting so weird?"

"I should call Mom and let her know we're ok."

"I called her from the payphone in the office when I got the key."

I got under the covers. I couldn't understand why I felt that afraid. I rolled onto my side near the edge of the bed.

"Goodnight," he said. He didn't bother to turn off the light.

3:33 flashed on the clock on the bedside table when I opened my eyes. The light was still on. I could hear trucks passing on the highway. The TV was on. It was old, and the colors on the screen had an orange glow. Then, I felt Pop's hand on my stomach. I felt him press his body into mine.

"Elena, are you sleeping?" His breath was hot on my skin.

3:34. I clutched my pillow tighter as his hand went beneath the elastic of my pajama pants, and then beneath the thin fabric of my underwear. His hands were rough, the skin hard.

"No, Pop."

"Relax, sweetheart."

I inhaled the stench of his breath. His fingers pushed inside me. I cried out and tried to swat his hand away, but he took it and placed it on himself. I yanked my hand away.

I prayed he would stop. I squeezed my eyes and tears fell onto my pillow and I smelled my mother on it, my bedroom. Home.

He pulled away. I didn't know whether I should pull up my pants or wait 'til he fell asleep. I was too scared to move.

At 3:41, the volume on the TV grew louder.

This time when he touched me he moaned.

"Stop crying," he said, but I couldn't. My sobs muffled his noises. I wished he would just beat me instead. Choke me like he did my mother. Kill me. I wanted to die.

Blood seeped from my bottom lip as I bit down on it. I tasted it with the tears that collected at the corner of my lips. His breath was all over me.

Laughter rattled from the television. I squinted and saw a Nesquik chocolate milk commercial on the screen. The children were happy. The brown bunny had floppy ears.

"Mija, trust me."

It all felt suffocating: his grunts and the dirty carpet and the dark room and the screech of the bed springs and the tires of the trucks on the highway and my tears and my blood—me—and his sour breath and Mom, so far away.

Elena, Elena: my name from his mouth.

The next morning, Pop was up before I was, putting on his shoes as he sat in a chair.

"Go get ready. We have to hit the road. I'll wait for you in the car."

I cried in the shower. I wanted to scrub myself with a wire pad until I bled. I got dressed in the bathroom with the door locked.

We didn't speak in the car except for when we were waiting to order food at a drive-thru. "I don't know what got into me," he said and paused for a second. "It was a mistake. We don't

need to tell Lovie or your mom." A voice crack-
led through the speaker outside the car window.
"Want some eggs?" he asked. I shook my head.

When we got to Florida, Lovie had a cheese
sandwich waiting for me. She smiled and gave
me a hug, and although I used to be angry at her
for taking my father away, I cried in her arms.

"How was the trip?" she asked, wiping my
eyes. "You must miss your mom."

I slept most of the week there, on the couch
of their cramped one-bedroom apartment. My
father barely said anything to me and instead
took double shifts at the local hospital, where he
worked as a security guard.

A week later, I flew home. Pop and Lovie
drove me to the airport. He patted me on the
back and said goodbye. On the plane, I felt safe
for the first time in days.

When Mom met me at the airport, her eyes
were red and swollen. She hugged me tight in
the middle of a crowd of people trying to step
around us to get to their bags.

"Mom, I have to tell you something."

She held me closer and whispered, "Your father called and told me what happened. Let's talk
about it in the car."

We walked in silence, except for the hum

of my suitcase rolling along the slick, polished floor. In the car on the way home, I stared out the window.

"I'm so sorry," Mom said. I turned to look at her. Her knuckles were white on the steering wheel. "You don't ever have to go see him again. I promise you that. It's over now. That's what's important."

"I can't believe he told you. He told me not to say anything," I started to cry.

"He said he knew you would tell me and didn't want things to get confused. That he was drunk, you guys were in the same bed, he thought you were Lovie, but then stopped." Mom put her hand back on the wheel.

"That's not true. He wasn't drunk. He knew it was me."

Mom exhaled, long and slow. "Look, he said he's sorry. We just need to let this go. It's over. Everything is over." As she said this, she didn't look at me.

"He did more. He knew what he was doing, Mom. We should tell someone. Don't you believe me?"

"Stop, Elena, please. We aren't telling anyone. How am I supposed to support both of us without his help?" We drove past an outdoor ice-skating rink, brightly lit and crowded with people. "You're never going to see or talk to him again, and no one is to ever know. And don't go telling your grandparents. It would destroy them."

I stared at the headlights illuminating the dark street ahead of us.

"Let's forget about it, ok?" she said.

I said nothing, and she fell silent, and that's the way it was for a long time.

It took nearly fifteen years for her to mention it again.

"I know I haven't been the best mom, but I want you to know I tried," she said. Her fingers rubbed against the handle of her suitcase.

"You don't want to miss your flight, Mom. Larry's going to wonder why his new wife didn't get off the plane," I joked, but she didn't laugh.

"Forgive me."

"Mom, it's not like you're dying. You're just moving across the country," I said, but I didn't look at her. 'Forgive me' were words she had never said before and they seemed to peel back that moment I took so long to bury.

"Please forgive me, Elena. I couldn't raise you on just my factory check, but now . . . " She began to cry.

"You need to go, Mom. Don't miss your flight."

"Why won't you talk about this?"

"You're asking me why I don't want to talk about this? In the middle of a damn airport?" Some people in line turned and glared at us. "Look," I said, my voice lower. "You go live your life, now. I'm grown. You've been the best mom you thought you could be, but don't ask me to forgive you for that."

"But, why?"

"Because I can't. Not yet."

"I love you. I'm sorry," she said, and turned to get into the security checkpoint line.

"Me too," I muttered, but she didn't hear me.

The funeral home seemed to shrink as more people arrived. The priest stood at the front of the room and began to speak.

I looked at my father. "I remember," I said.

"I don't know what . . . " he started, but he knew. His eyes darted around the room, but didn't meet mine.

"You think I'd just forget?" My heart hammered. We weren't in that funeral home anymore. We were back in that motel room. I could smell his breath and feel his hands on me again.

In that second, I saw my reflection in his eyes.

I looked just like him. The same wide mouth, the same brown, thick hair. For years, I hated that I resembled the person I hated most in the world.

Grandpa hooked his arm with mine, breaking the silence. "I know you two don't talk, but I love you both, so you got to at least respect each other for me. I want to be at peace with whatever time I have left. I ask you both to give me that."

Grandpa was the father I never had and I wanted to tell him what happened to me; to hate his son as much as I hated him, but I couldn't bring myself to say anything. The time to save me was long gone.

HOW WE GOT HERE

When I was little, Mom, Dad, and I ate at Frank's Pizzeria almost every Friday night. Afterward, we'd go home to watch a movie before bed. After Dad's car accident, we kept it up. He would have wanted us to. That first Friday without him, just after the fifth grade, Mom and I sat on the couch and watched Dad's empty recliner instead of the TV, like we expected him to appear there or something.

The Friday before Mom's 53rd birthday, I waited for her at Frank's in a booth that faced a family laughing at something I couldn't hear. I got a call from a number I didn't recognize. The man on the other line said, *Your mother has been sexually assaulted.*

I don't remember how I got to the hospital. If it wasn't for the keys that I squeezed so tight in my fist the metal pierced my skin, I would have guessed I had *thought* myself there.

Mom was in a bed with a steel frame covered in a sheet so thin I could see the blue dots on her hospital gown underneath. A doctor, a nurse, and two police officers were talking in hushed voices on one side of the room.

"Mija," she whispered. I took a few steps toward her. White strands of her hair wilted on her forehead. Her eyes were dull, and her lips quivered, but she managed to smile.

"We're done for now. We'll leave you two alone," the doctor said, and led everyone out of the room. The nurse stopped to fold in the steel stirrups on the bed, and covered Mom's feet with the sheet. One of the officers folded his small notebook and put it in his pocket. The other held a white crisp bag in his hand.

"Mom," was all I could say. I grabbed her hand, which felt as cold as the room, and she grabbed back. All I could do was kneel next to her, our hands connected between the bars of the steel frame, and not let go.

Mom never went back to her apartment. She stayed with me that night and every night that followed. She didn't talk about what happened. Only that it had happened a block away from her place. The only description she'd been able to give to the police of her attacker was a Latino male in his early twenties, mustache. It sounded like over half of the guys in her neighborhood.

She broke her lease and moved into my place. One night, after she took two of the sleeping pills the doctors prescribed her, I went to her apartment. I packed up what I thought she'd want to keep with her: the framed pictures that stood on the living room table, her clothes, her plants, and arranged for everything else to go into storage.

I was making my final trip out to the car with the last box when I noticed a man standing on the sidewalk in front of the apartment building. I felt him take in my entire body, from my gym shoes, my sweats, up to the box in my arms, and then his eyes met mine. I kept walking. The box was heavy, and I staggered to my car.

He was young, Latino, and was sprouting a mustache that curled upward. I wanted to heave him down onto the ground, drop the box on his head. I wanted to line up every man in that neighborhood, crush skull after skull with box after box until they were all gone.

The nurse had said they washed the dirt and blood from my mother twice, that she had cried both times. She had called this reaction *normal*.

"You need help with that?" he asked. I glared

at him. The box banged into the others as I put it in the trunk.

Those first few months, Mom didn't leave my apartment. Instead, she quit her job and stayed inside lying in bed or cleaning the kitchen counter until the granite shined like glass in the dark. My windows were so clean I could finally see my reflection in them.

Every night when I got home from work, Mom had dinner ready. I always asked about her day. She always responded, "Better than yesterday," but I never did believe her.

"If you ever want to talk about it, Mom . . . " I'd try.

She would shake her head and put her hand on mine. "Thank you, mija, but not now."

I don't know if it was because she didn't want to remember, or if she was trying to protect us from what might happen if we talked about it. I would have listened to every word, and yet, I felt relief when she didn't say anything. I didn't know if I could handle hearing what had been done to her.

Almost a year later, we were called in to a suspect lineup at the police station. The ten-minute drive felt more like ten days. My mother's hands never left her lap. She'd lost a lot of weight in the last year and her sweater hung loosely from her small frame.

"What happens if I don't recognize him?" she asked without looking at me. Her eyes were closed.

"Everything will be ok," I said, having no idea if it was true.

I pulled into the station's parking lot. Mom opened her eyes and took a deep breath. "Everything will be ok, Mom," I said again, taking her arm and slipping it through mine. She held onto me. If not for her sweater against my bare arm, I wouldn't have felt her there.

As the door opened, we were bombarded with screeching telephones, laughter, shouting, babies crying, and one single, "How can I help you?"

Mom squeezed my hand, her nails in my palm. She leaned into me, and asked, "What happens if it *is* him?"

It wasn't him. So, another year passed. Mom met with a therapist. She'd begun having nightmares, many nights of no sleep, and bouts of anger and frustration. As calls and visits from the detectives diminished, so did our hope that he would ever be caught.

One Friday night that winter, when the snow fell so that the streets looked like they were covered in a sheet of sugar, I came home from work to find dinner, as usual: rice steaming off the plate and baked chicken.

"How was your day, Mom?"

And then, finally, she told me everything.

I listened, even though it hurt my insides, and I wondered about *her insides* and how much they must hurt, *still*. And when she was done, I knelt beside her like I had in the hospital room, clutching her hand, crying in her lap as she caressed my head, and I couldn't tell who was holding whom anymore.

ALL THAT'S LEFT

On the plane ride to Guatemala, you seemed
more like a nervous child than a twenty-five-
year-old woman. During takeoff, you held onto
my arm, your head on my shoulder. Your long
hair fell down my neck and across my breasts.
I knew you didn't like flying, but you said you
wanted to go with me anyway. Visit another
country and meet my grandma, whom I'd been
visiting for two weeks every summer since I was
ten. *We've been friends for so long. It's about time we
took a real trip together*, you said.

At hour three, you got a little more anxious
and grabbed my hand, your knees shaking. Your
hand felt so familiar in mine.

"Are you alright?"

"It's just stupid. I need to—" You never finished.

You let go of my hand and turned to face out
the window. I leaned, looked out, and saw only
clouds. I thought of the game we played when

we were younger, when we'd find turtles and balloons and cows in the clouds. But we weren't kids anymore. Now, they were just clouds.

"You're thinking about him," you said, still looking out the window.

"When am I not?"

"You need to let go."

"I know."

When we landed, my grandma said we were the prettiest young ladies she had ever seen. When I introduced you, I told her in Spanish that you and I had been best friends since fourth grade. She told me in return to treasure it because one didn't find friends like that anymore.

I knew you didn't have a grandma, not one you ever knew. From that moment on, I shared my grandma with you.

Remember that during the drive into town, we saw that dog the color of horchata limping down the dirt road? We could see his ribs under his thin skin. "My heart hurts for him," you said.

Grandma took us to the mercado, where we bought those strapless dresses—mine green, yours yellow—and matching straw flip-flops, and barrettes shaped like papayas and mangos, and wooden necklaces of the Mayan Sun God. We paid more for it all than the old lady had asked.

"You're beautiful, really," you told me as we waited to cross the street. Our dresses flapped in the warm breeze, and I thought about how I wished *he* had said the same.

Then there was the earthquake. The one we exercised through. After just a week of inhaling Grandma's home cooking, we almost couldn't fit into the clothes that we had brought. So, we hopped around to a kickboxing VHS we found in her attic. We giggled through the whole thing. Grandma got up and peeked into the living room. She watched us and grinned. We smiled back, not aware of the tremors for a moment.

The next day she said she hadn't wanted to scare us when the earthquake happened. It hadn't been a strong one, but it was felt by every other person in Guatemala City, every dog and chicken and horse. But not by us. We were somewhere else.

Over the next several days, we lingered on a beach with black sand. We ate fresh fish from the ocean, but we requested the heads to be cut off because we didn't want to see their faces. We ignored the cat-calling from men shorter than us who carried machetes at their sides and wore hats so big their faces masked in shadows. We even climbed the pyramids in the middle of the jungle. When we got to the top we shared a sandwich and soda.

"I'm happy to be here with you," you said, then wrapped your arms around me.

"Me too."

The night before heading back home, we sat on the roof of Grandma's house, encased in the heat. We could see the volcanoes veiled in darkness miles away. We watched one spurt red-orange lava, liquid fire.

That's when you told me that you loved me.

"I love you too," I said.

"No, I really love you."

I heard horses trotting down the dirt road and could smell tortillas baking somewhere nearby. Some men on the street spoke in Spanish about cerveza and a cantina.

"I love you like you love him."

You held my hand, twining each of your fingers with mine. You said it again: "I love you."

Someone played cumbias that echoed into the street. The marimbas and the guitar swirled around us. I rubbed my leg, irritating my sunburn.

You gazed at my hand in yours.

"Look at me."

I did.

"I know you don't feel the same, but I love you anyway."

You let go of my hand.

The next morning, we said goodbye to Grandma and took a cab to the airport. When I tried to hold your hand on the plane, you pulled away.

Instead, you watched the clouds.

GET IT ON

It wasn't that Sebastian was ashamed of his wife, Grace, who was seven months pregnant with twins. It was just that before the pregnancy, her body used to fit into tight jeans, and even tighter sweaters, curves his tongue and his fingers traced like a roller coaster, up and down and around. It was just different now. No, Sebastian wasn't ashamed of Grace. He just no longer wanted to have sex with her.

Sebastian met Grace at her thirtieth birthday party with a mutual friend. He knew by the way she smiled at him and let him touch the curve of her back as they spoke that he had to be with her. Her tank top hugged her breasts and wrapped around her flat stomach. Her jeans seemed to have been painted onto her round ass and thick thighs. She was a dream to him. They spoke about books they each were reading and he told her she would love her thirties. He had just turned thirty himself and look where that got him. She smiled.

Grace was beautiful, smart, and willing to have sex in more places and in more positions than anyone else he'd ever been with. Even after they were married, they had sex four to five times a week. A few days without it and they'd both refer to it as a drought. Grace was the only woman he had been with that he still fantasized about, and the only woman in his life that he never cheated on.

"I'm fat," Grace cried, yet again, at the breakfast table. Her hair was pulled up into a messy bun on top of her head. Her face, once oval-shaped and sharply angled, was now round and soft. She wore glasses over her tired eyes, and her lips were chapped.

"You're not fat, honey," Sebastian said, pouring coffee into a mug as he turned away from her. His hair was as black as the coffee, his skin still wrinkleless. In the pocket of his dress pants he felt his car keys. He couldn't wait to get to work.

When they first found out she was pregnant, he didn't think twice about their sex life. Grace said it would go on as it always had, but the larger she got, he found it almost impossible to feel turned on by her.

"I'm ginormous," Grace said again. Tears gushed onto the pancakes in front of her. The sticky syrup dripped over the plate onto the wooden table.

"You're not ginormous," Sebastian muttered, stirring sugar into his coffee.

He didn't hear her waddle her way over to him. He was continuously surprised at how silent she was on her swollen feet. She put her hand on his shoulder and he jumped.

"You know what would make me feel better?" she said. Her belly nudged his abs. He swore he felt the twins kicking in objection. Her chest began to heave. Her body shielded the light from the window. *An eclipse in the middle of my kitchen*, Sebastian thought.

"I'm late, Grace," Sebastian said, side-stepping her. She eyeballed him. She massaged her stomach in little circles.

"You don't find me desirable anymore, do you?"

"Of course, I do, sweetheart. I'm just late and you know how I feel about, you know."

"Stop with that. I told you nothing is going to happen to the babies. You haven't had sex with me in ages. Do you know how crazy my hormones are right now?"

"Grace, c'mon," Sebastian said, as he inched by her.

"Fine, go. But I have needs, Sebastian Friedman."

Sebastian yanked his coat off the hook and fled through the door.

Sebastian would sometimes grab coffee from the café under the L tracks. Next to the café was Gigi's Porn Shop. To the door of the shop was taped a small cardboard sign that read *Adults Only. Cash Only.* Grace and Sebastian had gone to sex shops before, but not this one. Grace didn't mind them at all, as long as they went together.

Sebastian caught his reflection in the windows, which he later found out worked as a one-way mirror, so he could see the people on the street, but they couldn't see him. The bell rang from above the door as Sebastian made his way in. At first all he saw was spine after spine of adult films on the shelves by the door.

"It's a dollar to look," Sebastian heard a woman say. The shop was small and the counter was near enough to him that he could read the young woman's shirt, *I Like Men With Big Vocabularies.* He had never seen a woman work any sex shop counter before, yet there she was with her

long dark hair and large lips and that tiny waist.
She reminded him of someone.

She looked like Grace.

Well, like Grace *used* to look.

He felt something stir in him, specifically
in his pants, and muttered, "Oh, I don't carry
cash," and hurried out of the shop. As the door
closed, he heard the woman say, "Next time."
Sebastian walked back to his office building,
thinking he hadn't been that excited in awhile.
He had needs, too.

After work, Sebastian dragged his feet to the
house and hesitated before turning the key in
the door. He knew Grace wanted to get it on and
he didn't know what to say this time. Over the
last few months he had overused the following
excuses: I'm too tired, aren't you too tired? I
have a headache, don't you have a headache? I
don't want to hurt the babies, how can you be
so sure it won't hurt the babies? I have to work
from home tonight. I have to fix the leaky faucet.
I have to mow the lawn. I have to feed the dog
(even though they didn't actually own a dog).

The house was calm, the lights off, and he
remembered it was Tuesday, when Grace had
her Mommy-To-Be class over at the Y. Tuesdays

were his favorite. He'd get down to his boxers, open up his laptop, and search for a porno
to watch.

For the last six weeks, while Grace was in
class learning how to care for her soon-to-be
babies, Sebastian was caring for himself. Sometimes in that moment, when although he knew
Grace wasn't coming home anytime soon, he
still held in his moans. He usually thought
of the old her, or the women in the pornos,
but tonight he had the woman from Gigi's on
his mind.

Sebastian was hard already, thinking of what
was to come, feeling a little guilty, but not
enough to think twice about it. He went to the
bedroom to take off his clothes.

In the middle of their bed was a pamphlet
with *Sebastian* scribbled in black marker above
the title: *A Husband's Complete Guide to Pregnancy
Sex*. The pamphlet was pale orange with two
stick figures, one with a round belly, sitting on
a bed holding stick hands. He immediately felt
himself soften and picked up the pamphlet. A
post-it note said, "I have needs too, Sebastian
Freidman."

Sebastian sat on the bed and opened the
pamphlet.

Sexual Positions During Pregnancy

As she grows, the traditional man-on-top position is more uncomfortable for pregnant women. The pregnant woman should not be flat on her back because the growing uterus can compress major blood vessels.

"Great," Sebastian murmured. He looked at the next page. Stick figures accompanied each position.

Try the following instead:

Have Her Get on Top! *This position has been shown to be associated with higher levels of sexual satisfaction in pregnant women. It puts no weight on her abdomen and allows her to control the depth of penetration.*

When Grace got home from class that night, she found Sebastian perched on the bed, the pamphlet propped up on the nightstand.

"Oh, Seb," she said, and came over to him. Sebastian forced a smile. He remembered the girl back at the shop, her perky boobs stretching the words on her shirt like a billboard. He leaned in and kissed Grace, thinking of that woman. It managed to get him hard enough and he lay back on the bed.

"Get on top," he said.

Grace clapped her hands twice like she was

a cheerleader at the big game. She wiggled out of her maternity clothes. Sebastian lay there, his eyes closed, trying to stay decently hard. He felt the bed bounce. He heard her breathe heavy and moan a bit. *Well, this isn't so bad*, he thought.

Grace panted, "I'm not feeling so well. Help me get off . . . you know what I mean."

That wasn't the getting off Sebastian had in mind.

"I'll be good to try again in a few minutes. I really want this," she said, as she walked to the dresser. She picked up a bottle of cocoa butter and began rubbing it over her stretch marks.

Sebastian now really wanted to get off, but not with Grace. While she took a call from her mother in the living room, he took a shower, and took care of himself. When Grace tried again, he apologized, but he'd just lost it. Falling asleep, he thought about making another trip to Gigi's tomorrow. This time he'd bring cash.

The chime of the bell was silenced this time by the train roaring over Gigi's. Sebastian's hand was in his pocket, rubbing the dollar bill between his fingers. A man in a blue uniform looked up when he walked in, then turned his attention to the stack of movies he was juggling in his hands.

When Sebastian spotted her, he walked past the movies and went straight to the counter. This time she was wearing a plain white shirt that showed off her cleavage. She was reading *The Great Gatsby*.

"Here's my dollar," he said, leaning on the counter.

"You get it back if you buy something," she said. No smile, not even a glance. Then she reached out her hand across the glass near his. Sebastian waited for this woman who looked like his wife but less pregnant to touch his hand. He felt himself getting hard.

"Don't lean on the counter." She tapped the glass. Beneath Sebastian was a sign that read, *Do Not Lean on Glass*.

"Oh, sorry," he said, jerking away. Embarrassed, he pretended to look around the small shop quickly, and then left the store.

When Sebastian got home, he saw the pamphlet once again, this time on the nightstand. He wasn't a quitter. He heard the shower running and Grace humming.

He opened up the pamphlet:

Lie side-by-side in the spoon position. *This allows for only shallow penetration. Deep thrusts can become uncomfortable as the months pass.*

"How was work, honey?" Grace asked, her hair dripping. Her towel looked tiny wrapped around her body.

"Get on your side on the bed. We're trying this again," he said, tossing the pamphlet back on the nightstand. Grace sighed, but walked around the bed and lay on her side facing away from him. Sebastian focused on the birthmark on her lower back that he'd always loved. It was the shape of the Philippines and the color of lightly toasted bread. He thought this would help him forget the two squatters in her stomach.

Sebastian got inside. He thought of his twins and how they were probably crammed in there next to one another with their knee-less legs crossed like they were meditating, their hands underneath their non-existent chins, shaking their heads and rolling their eyes.

"Sebastian, I'm not comfortable," Grace said. Sebastian pulled out and rolled over on his back. "Thanks, though. I'm just not in the mood," she said.

"But, you're *always* in the mood," he said. After weeks of pestering him, he was finally ready and willing to sleep with Grace, and now she wasn't in the mood?

"What's the big deal? You never want to anyway," she said, and went to the bathroom to blow dry her hair.

That night while she slept, Sebastian dreamt he was in Gigi's Porn Shop. That woman was naked reading *The Great Gatsby* standing behind the counter, but he couldn't get to her. A disembodied voice was repeating, *No leaning on the counter.*

This time Sebastian had the dollar out and ready, and when he gave it to that woman, he was going to get her name and make small talk. Tell her his name in hopes that she would repeat it, so he could carry the sound of his name from her mouth for later that evening.

Instead, behind the counter there was a heavy man with a thick beard, drinking a diet soda and laughing at some cartoon on the small TV near him.

"It's a dollar, mister."

"I don't carry cash," Sebastian said. He thrust the dollar into his pocket and walked back out onto the street.

When Sebastian got home that night, Grace was napping on the recliner. She looked so peaceful, almost beautiful. He was good and ready to go, and thinking about another woman was better than actually cheating. He plucked the pamphlet from their bedroom and read over the other positions:

Make love sitting down. *This is another position that puts no weight on her uterus. Sit on a (sturdy) chair and have her straddle you. She can control the rate and depth of penetration by standing up more or by squatting down.*

Oral sex safe during pregnancy

Normal oral sex won't harm her or your baby. In fact, it can be a good solution if intercourse is deemed too risky. The only thing you must avoid is blowing air into her vagina. Blowing air can cause a blockage of a blood vessel by an air bubble (known as an air embolism). An embolism can be potentially fatal for her and your baby.

Get her onto her hands or knees in the doggy position. *This is a good position for later on in her pregnancy when it's a relief to have weight taken off her pelvis. Penetration can be quite deep in this position.*

If she finds it uncomfortable, hold a pillow between her bottom and your lower tummy. This will prevent you from pushing too far inside her.

Sebastian marched down the hallway and tapped Grace on the shoulder a few times. She yawned.

"Let's go," he said, and clutched her hand to help her up.

"Now?" she said, half asleep.

Eventually, they got to the bedroom.

"Get on your knees." He pointed to the bed, undoing his belt.

"You have such a way with words," Grace said, yawning again.

"You used to love this position."

"It's been so long, I forgot," she said. "Why are you putting a pillow under my ass?"

"So, I don't penetrate too deep or something."

He was going to satisfy his wife. He'd always had and he wasn't going to stop now. He was behind her and about to enter her when he heard it.

Grace was snoring.

He pulled back. Grace's face was on another pillow, her mouth open.

"Grace!" he said. She snorted and woke up.

"What?" she rolled to her side and struggled to sit up. She saw him standing there, exposed and soft. "I'm sorry. I'm exhausted."

Sebastian snickered.

"Wait," Grace said. "You don't have sex with

me for months, you make me feel undesirable while I'm carrying *your* babies, and then the few times I don't want it, you make a big deal out of it?"

Sebastian didn't know what to say. He put his boxers back on and sat next to her on the bed.

"I gave you that pamphlet to let you know that the babies would be safe. To prove a point. I want us to have sex when we do because we both want to be with the other. I thought that pamphlet would help, but without it you never made an effort to be with me."

Sebastian stared at the carpet. "I'm sorry," he said. Then he kissed her, and Grace kissed him back, and this time when he touched her, his hands going to places that made her quiver, she didn't fall asleep.

The next morning he walked to the café and stopped in front of Gigi's Porn Shop. He stood in between the two, the porn shop on his left, and the café on his right. A couple of dollars in his pocket.

He entered the café.

THE VISIT

When Alex told me he had kissed someone else, we were at our favorite 24-hour diner, the one near our place. The one that we had been going to for hash browns and omelets since we had started dating over two years ago.

"Emily, I didn't mean for it to happen. I'm sorry," he said as the waitress came and put the plates of food in front of us. She darted her eyes between us, threw two straws on the table, and hurried away.

I think he expected me to yell or to cry, but instead I reached for the hot sauce and shook bright orange drops of it onto the food.

"Aren't you going to say anything?" Alex's hand slid towards mine, but then he took it back.

I didn't know what to say. It's not like I was purely innocent either, but was now the time to tell him? *Hey, Alex. You know a couple of months ago when I went to that conference in San Diego? I fucked my counterpart from Tucson, the one that I had never met in person before.*

"It didn't mean anything. It just happened." He tapped his fingers against the tabletop. My water quaked inside the glass.

"Maybe we've hit our max," I said, putting butter on my toast.

"Max?"

"You should eat. It's getting cold," I pointed to his plate with my fork.

"Why are you being like this? Can't you have some kind of reaction?" Alex leaned over the table and put his hands flat in front of me, but didn't try to touch me.

"I need time to think. I don't know about us."

"It was just a kiss," he said, but I wasn't referring to that. I didn't know where Alex and I had gone wrong. I wasn't sure if I even wanted to fix it.

The next day we rode the train to the airport. It was packed with travelers and suitcases all piled in tightly like toys in a chest. I knew Grandma Helen was going to ask where Alex was. He'd come with me the last two summers to visit her and Grandpa Edmond.

Alex and I decided that if I could get over his

indiscretion, as he put it, then I would call him to join me. If not, that would mean the end of us.

"Know that I want you to call me and tell me to come," Alex said, holding my carry-on bag over his shoulder as he leaned against the train door. I pointed to my ear and shook my head, pretending I couldn't hear him over the all the conversations and the loud roar of the train.

We didn't speak the rest of the way and when we got to the terminal, we did not hug. I took my bag from him.

"I'm sorry," Alex said.

"I'll call you by six o'clock and let you know," I replied, and made my way to security.

I got to Grandma Helen's ranch house on Montrose Avenue at two o'clock in the afternoon. I stood on the sidewalk in front of the house, my feet planted on top of my own initials, which I'd etched into the sidewalk when I was a kid. I still wasn't sure if I was going to tell Alex to come or not. At that point, all I knew was that I needed to talk to Grandma Helen about it. She'd give it to me straight.

The gnomes that lined the walkway to Grandma's house seemed to sweat in the broiling sun as I made my way up the walkway to the door. I hadn't seen her since Grandpa Edmond's funeral nearly a year before, when the house was full of people and casseroles.

Grandma opened the door before I even had a chance to ring the bell. A blast of cold air pulled me inside. Grandma Helen stood almost as high as the side table, her hair puffed up like a croissant. Her two Great Danes trotted up to me, sniffing my knees as if they were biscuits.

After several minutes of hugs, Grandma led me into the house. It was the same as it had always been—plants on every shelf of the bookcase, the green couch covered in plastic that pulled at your skin when you sat on it. When my grandparents had watched me when I was a child, I'd learned to sneak some cookies to Grandpa to snack on while we watched horror movies on that very couch. I watched the scary parts through the gaps of my fingers as I covered my eyes.

"Emily, dear, it's Grandpa's Santa suit. Put it on." Grandma said, coming into the room. She placed a wad of red cloth into my bare arms. Immediately, my white tank was covered in red fibers.

"It's August, Grandma, and I wanted to talk about something."

"What? We can only celebrate the birth of Jesus once a year? C'mon, dear. Your Grandpa Edmond and I would always do a test run of the Christmas card this time of year."

I recalled all the various cards I had received, each with Grandpa Edmond in a Santa suit and Grandma Helen dressed like Mrs. Claus or a snowman. Once she was even an elf. Grandpa filled out the suit early on, but it sagged more and more as the years had gone on and he became sicker. Then one of the dogs came along a couple years ago and a reindeer started appearing in the cards, too.

"But, I don't want to, Grandma," I said, sounding more like I was four instead of thirty-four.

"You don't have to if you don't want to. I mean, I'm all alone now. Your grandpa is gone. Your dad's off in Alaska and you, so many states away . . . " Grandma let go of Grandpa Edmond's Santa suit. It fell to the rug.

She began to tremble. "I don't feel well. Oh, Lawd, my dear Jesus," she moaned.

Dad had warned me that Grandma Helen had started acting sick when she didn't get her way. Now that Grandpa was in an urn on top of the kitchen table, she didn't have anyone to pay attention to her anymore.

"Fine. fine. I'll put on the suit." I trudged over and scooped it up. Grandma immediately stopped moaning.

"Oh, such a sweetheart, so unlike your father," she chirped. Dad was her only child. "Let me go get the camera he sent me for Mother's Day, since he just couldn't bring himself to come see me."

"Mom and Dad are in Alaska because of his job, remember?" I yelled after her.

"What's a little plane ride from Alaska to Chicago?" she said, her voice fading.

I plopped on the couch, the plastic crinkling beneath me. During one visit Alex had fallen asleep on it, and his face stuck to the plastic.

One of the Great Danes pranced over to me. "How you doing, Oscar?" I said, petting him behind his ear. It was still odd for me to call the dog Oscar. He was named after my dad. They both did have slightly tilted ears.

The other Dane strolled over to me. He was leaner; his shoulders moved back and forth like oars.

"And how are you, Edmond?" I said. I scratched him on the top of his head. Grandma had gotten him after Grandpa died.

The dogs sat next to each other, gazing at me,

the sunlight from the open blinds shining over their charcoal fur.

On the table, which Grandpa had made himself, stood a nearly empty spray bottle. On its label was a picture of a Labrador wearing sunglasses and sitting underneath a palm tree. I bent down and sniffed Edmond's head. He smelled like coconuts.

"Smell like Hawaii, don't they?" Grandma said, coming back into the room. "They say dogs and coconuts are good for arthritis."

"I didn't know you had arthritis."

"I don't. It's a preventative measure."

She raised her furry brows at me. At 86, Grandma Helen was still pretty sharp. She remembered when her soap operas were on, and how she met Grandpa Edmond in the fifties, and when others forgot her birthday.

"Well, are you going to put it on or what?" she asked me.

Grandpa Edmond was such a tall man that my little five-foot-flat grandma never had to climb a ladder or a step stool in her married life. She'd just scream, "Edmond!" and he'd get whatever she wanted from the top shelf. Grandpa had to bend over to kiss her on the top of her head.

I glanced at my watch. Time was ticking away and I was still not sure what I was going to do about Alex. I slid the Santa pants on over my own without removing my shoes. I kept tugging and tugging and my shoes never seemed to peek out. There were suspenders on the waistband that I hung over my shoulders.

I imagined Grandpa laughing at me as I struggled. When I was little he'd sneak me candy before bed and after bed, before dinner and after dinner, and sometimes during dinner. I missed him. I could almost smell the Old Spice within the fibers of the Santa suit.

Alex had taken the phone call when he died.

"My poor grandma. They've been together for so long," I cried.

"I'm lucky to have you," Alex had said.

The great Danes studied me, turning their heads slightly. The coat alone was almost at my knees and it itched like crazy over my tank top. The coat fibers were prickling my skin and I began to squirm.

"Oh, how I wish your grandpa was here."

"Me too."

"You look beautiful, Emily. Now just sit down. No. No. In *his* chair," Grandma Helen pointed to

Grandpa Edmond's chair. I hadn't laid my eyes on it since I came in and now when I noticed it, I saw that his urn had moved from the kitchen to the dented plush cushion.

"It was next to the camera, dear," Grandma said. "Look, just sit there and put the urn in your lap."

"You want me to put Grandpa on my lap?"

I didn't mean to laugh, but I did. When I was a kid and sat on his lap, I never fathomed that I would be returning the favor.

Grandma began to cry, an all-out groaning, hyper-ventilating, chest-heaving, denture-quaking kind of a cry.

"I'm all alone," she moaned. The only other time I had seen Grandma so upset was at the funeral. Alex had held her, rubbing her back, telling me later that he could feel her spine as she curled into him. I was shaking hands and trying to get people through the house. How was I supposed to talk to her now? *Hey, Grandma. Sorry you're depressed, but let me tell you about my problem, so you can help me.*

The guilt started to shoot up my spine. I picked up the urn. Underneath my fingers, it was cool and smooth. I sat in the recliner and sunk into the dent of the cushion. The Danes instantly began to bark and trotted toward me. Edmond sat to my left and rested his massive head on my thigh and Oscar laid right smack on top of my feet. Grandma Helen yelped in delight and wiped the tears with the back of her hand.

"Thank you, Emily. Now the hat, dear." I scanned the room and didn't see a hat. Grandma Helen pointed to the coat.

"In the right pocket," she said.

I reached inside and pulled out a stiff stick of licorice covered in dog hair.

"My dear heavens, that man," she shook her head. "He shouldn't have been eating sweets because of his diabetes! They cut off his leg, you know."

"They didn't cut off his leg, Grandma."

"Well, they would've cut it off if it wasn't for me who stopped him from eating sweets." She turned her focus to the camera.

It occurred to me to tell her that the dogs didn't stop her from having arthritis, that Grandpa's leg didn't stay attached to his body because she monitored his sugar intake, but then she said, "Oh, wait. Didn't you want to talk about something? Is Alex on a later flight?"

I dropped the licorice to the floor and Oscar started sniffing it. Edmond seemed to want an answer to the question and peered up at me. I nervously rubbed my hands through my hair.

"Grandma, that's what I wanted to talk to you about," I said. I reached into the pocket again and grabbed a crumpled felt ball. I yanked the hat out. *Edmond* was written in glitter across the white rim, the last *d* almost completely worn away. I threw it on my head and it slid below my eyes. Grandma rolled up the rim of the hat until it squeezed my forehead.

"Let me just get one quick photo. Smile, dear. Oscar. Edmond. Look over here." The dogs turned their heads. I grinned, but I was thinking of Alex.

After the funeral, he had held Grandma's hand as she told him the story of how she and Grandpa Edmond first met, of when she had first seen him at the candy factory and knew she wasn't in love. They just got married because she had nothing else to do, but then she grew to love him. Alex joked about it later. Told me that we had it all backwards. We got together for love and that maybe it meant we'd end up apart.

"So, dear. Why didn't Alex come with you?" Grandma snapped a picture, but the camera was facing her, not me. She flipped it around.

"Because I need some time to think."

"Think about what?"

Snap. Oscar yawned.

"I need some time to figure things out."

"Words, dear. Words."

Another *snap.* This time Oscar's head was facing the door. Grandma Helen clicked her tongue and his head snapped toward her.

"Sometimes relationships aren't that easy, I guess."

"You're talking, but telling me nothing. I'm going to make us some tea, dear. That will help loosen your tongue."

And then, while wearing an itchy Santa suit, sitting on Grandpa's recliner, flanked by a pair of Great Danes, I told Grandma Helen about Alex.

"The butterflies are gone," I said as I came to the end. I had told her everything, even the cheating. She didn't ask for details and I was grateful for that.

"You sound like such a girl, Emily. Butterflies aren't forever. They fly and it feels fine and then they die." She sipped her tea.

"I love him. I do. I just am like *this* with him," I raised my hand and then swiped it straight across in the air.

"And you want this," she said, raising her free hand upward, like before the drop in a roller coaster. I nodded.

"Grandma, I don't want you to think I'm a bad person."

"Emily, look at me. You're my favorite grandchild."

"I'm your only grandchild."

"Still, I don't have to like you, dear, but I do. We're human. You just need to figure out what you want for yourself. I loved your grandpa more than anyone, but if I wasn't happy I would've left. Love isn't everything."

I didn't know what to say. I wanted to sink into the Santa suit even more, shrink until I was cocooned in it.

"Dear, your tea is getting cold." Grandma Helen pointed to my mug, then straightened out her skirt, pulling it over the dark veins that branched under her nude tights.

One of the dogs began to snore. The air conditioner blasted through the house, but sweat formed over my body.

"Your grandpa and I were together for forty-three years. We had an understanding. We were together because we wanted to be, not because we needed to. I don't believe in soul mates, dear, and I don't think you do, either. It's foolish to think there is only one person out there that you can be happy with. You need to figure that part out. Are you with Alex because you want to be, or do you feel that's the right thing to do? *There's nothing wrong with him, so why shouldn't I stay?* If you're thinking like that, it's not fair for either of you. Love is the foundation, but it's not the entire house. You need to ask yourself whether you want to spend the time and energy building it with him. It's a matter of not being scared and living, whether that means staying with Alex or moving on."

I rubbed my hands on my thighs. I still had the urn cradled upright in one arm. Both Danes were snoring at my feet.

"Things happen, dear, and not always in the way that you expect. Usually, never." She put the cup of tea down on the table and pushed herself up with the help of the recliner's arms. Her feet were silent on the carpet as she made her way to me. She put her hands on my face, warm and soft, and her eyes met mine.

"He was with someone else. You were with someone else. Make it work or walk away. It's your responsibility to make yourself happy, not someone else's."

"I know."

"Alex's not in this urn, Emily," she said, taking it from me and rubbing it like a genie's lamp. "Now, just a few more pictures, Emily dear. Let's wake up the dogs."

An hour later, after I had taken off the Santa suit and put it back in the closet, while Grandma prepared her famous potato salad and the Danes gnawed on bones that looked like they'd once belonged to dinosaurs, I called Alex.

After I hung up, I made my way into the kitchen. The Danes trailed behind me.

"Will Alex be joining us?" Grandma asked, putting a glass of lemonade in front of me. The ice clinked. The glass sweated. The dogs sat on either side of my chair.

"It's just you and me, Grandma."

She said nothing and kissed the top of my head.

We lounged on the deck and watched the Danes play in the backyard. The sun slowly dipped behind the fence until it disappeared.

NEXT IN LINE

Lloyd started working at the DMV right after high school. He'd wanted to study to be some kind of engineer, but when his mom moved out west to be with her fifth husband, he took the first job that was offered to him so he wouldn't have to go with her. That was twenty years ago.

Lloyd began as the person who set out the applications and made sure the seats were lined up just right, and moved to the person who took the pictures, then to the person who sat in the front and dealt with people who were angry because of the long wait. Now, he administered the driving tests. After a few years of minor accidents (mainly with teenagers who would bite their nails nervously and always forgot to signal), he had succumbed to the reality that this was the way it would always be. He'd work at the DMV 'til the day he hit retirement, or until the day he died. Whichever came first.

Lloyd followed a strict process for each test. He walked once around the car to inspect brake lights, headlights, and turn signals, frowning slightly, as if observing some kind of art he didn't quite understand. He took note of the car's cleanliness, determining if he could see the reflection of his legs and feet in the paint. Then he'd open the passenger door and check the seat. He learned early on that people didn't necessarily keep their seats clean. The test usually took less than ten minutes, which was just about as long as Lloyd could stand. In most vehicles, Lloyd's knees met the glove box.

"Hey, Lloyd, praying for no Mini Coopers today?" his co-workers teased.

"That's very clever. I should write that one down, but I don't need to. You'll use the same joke tomorrow," Lloyd replied.

The test took place on a course built on the DMV lot. It had a stop sign and a yield sign, a left and right hand turn, a track that went in a loop, and of course a parallel parking spot. It was short, but still allowed Lloyd to determine whether or not to pass a driver.

As the driver, young or old, man or woman, put his or her hands on the wheel, Lloyd would say, "Proceed," without much emotion, and then wouldn't say anything else.

The driver would either do a decent job and pass, or fail miserably, and it was all the same to Lloyd. He was there to do a job, to collect a paycheck, so he could go home and be alone.

On a Tuesday morning, right as the thunderstorm warning was announced, Lloyd prepared for his first driver of the day. He scanned down the list in his hand and yelled, "Melanie Lorenzo!" From the waiting area walked the most beautiful woman he had ever seen. Her sleeveless short summer dress revealed tiny freckles blossoming on her skin. Her hair was long and straight, dark as charcoal, and she wore thick-framed, purple glasses. Lloyd gazed at her, then caught himself. He signaled for her to follow him outside. He didn't hear a woman yell that there was no damn way she failed the written test. He didn't hear a baby crying while his mother waited in line, didn't hear the *click, click, click* of the pictures being taken at the booth or the phones ringing behind the desk. He heard only the slight smack of Melanie's flip-flops and the clink of what must have been coins shifting in her purse, as if she carried a loaded piggy bank inside. She walked up to him and grinned.

"You're probably wondering why it took a

thirty-five-year-old so long to learn how to drive, huh? Everyone else waiting for the test isn't even old enough to drink." She laughed. "I mean, good morning."

Lloyd watched her lips move. He thought they were the color of raspberries.

"Let's proceed," he said, gripping the clipboard tightly. Had he still been married, his ring would have dug into his skin. "Which car is yours?"

Melanie pointed to a small blue car with a white stripe along the side. He couldn't see his reflection in the car, but that didn't matter right now. She dug around in her purse and pulled out her keys. They were attached to a keychain of a topless woman swimming in blue waves.

"Dumb Peter. It's his car. He's waiting in the coffee shop across the street."

"Peter is your dumb brother?" Lloyd asked, and then cringed. He was hoping Melanie wasn't holding her boyfriend's keys.

"Peter is my friend and not nearly as dumb as my brother."

Lloyd didn't know if he was supposed laugh at this.

Lloyd didn't even check the inside of the car. Instead, he dropped into the passenger seat and as Melanie settled inside the car, he noticed a tattoo that peeked from underneath her dress just below her shoulder. It looked like a vine in varied shades of gray. Lloyd despised tattoos—he thought them unwomanly. But Melanie's tattoo was beautiful. He wanted to lean over and look at it closely.

Big dark clouds began to gather in the sky as Melanie placed her hands at ten and two. "My mom never learned to drive because she was in a bad car accident when she was little and was too afraid. Growing up, we took the bus everywhere or just walked. She always said driving was too dangerous, but I've decided it's time I learned. Sometimes there's more danger in being afraid, right?" Melanie smiled. "But I am a little nervous."

Lloyd said, "Don't worry. You'll do great." Melanie smiled again. This was more than Lloyd had said to a driver in all his years at the DMV. "Proceed."

Melanie grinned.

Lloyd wanted to kiss her.

Melanie put the car in drive and crept forward. She glanced to her left, then her right, then her left, then her right. There was no other car on the course.

"Just go straight here, Miss Lorenzo," said Lloyd.

Melanie pressed the gas and approached the stop sign. Lloyd kept his eyes on her. He was in awe—the darkness of her hair, the beauty mark beneath her lip.

The car stopped.

"So far, so good, Miss Lorenzo," Lloyd said.

Lloyd hadn't dated anyone since his ex-wife left. She had worked at the DMV too. She made him feel special and for a few years he made her feel special, too. Then one day, there was someone else and she left. Since then, it had been difficult for him to meet anyone new.

"My wife left me," he blurted.

"Oh, I'm sorry," Melanie said. "I'm divorced too."

"I'm sorry," Lloyd replied. He wanted to reach over and grab her hand.

"I'm not," Melanie said, and made a perfect left turn. "Neither Bill or I were happy, but neither of us would do what we both knew needed to happen. It's like we had to wait to see who would go first."

Lloyd nodded. He watched her click on the right turn signal. Her fingers were long and thin, her nails shiny, unpainted, so he could see the pink of her skin underneath.

As Melanie made the turn, she said, "So, finally one day I had enough. It's not like either of us are bad people. We just weren't the right fit for each other."

Melanie looked over to read Lloyd's nametag. "Don't be so hard on yourself, Lloyd H. Okay? You seem a little sad." She briefly took one of her hands off the wheel and placed it on top of Lloyd's.

Lloyd felt her soft skin, the warmth of it.

It started to rain. Melanie returned her hand to the wheel and turned on the wipers. They squealed back and forth as she made the loop around the course. Lloyd wished the test would never end.

When she came to the parallel parking spot, Melanie sighed. "Ok, I've been practicing this a lot. Let's see how I do, Lloyd."

She backed into the parking space without a problem.

"Lloyd, look how good I parked, and in the rain! You're the expert—I'm good, no?" Melanie laughed and brushed his arm. Lloyd wanted to grab her hand, to feel it on top of his one more time.

"Miss Lorenzo," Lloyd began, and she told him to call her Melanie. "Melanie, very well. I have to tell you something." He took a deep breath.

He wanted to tell her he wanted to take her out. Anywhere. Somewhere they could talk, where he could get to know all about her: her tattoos, her friend Peter, how in the world her husband could let her go. He wanted to tell her how she made him aware of something he'd needed to understand—he didn't want to be alone.

"You passed," he said.

Melanie applauded. "It wasn't as hard as I thought! I heard the driving test was difficult, but you were really supportive. Thanks."

Inside the DMV, Lloyd watched Melanie have her picture taken. She stood at the counter for a moment when her new driver's license was handed to her. She rubbed it and smiled. When she looked across the room, her eyes met his and she waved, holding up the license.

"Remember what I said, Lloyd H. Sometimes it's just not the right fit," she called out, sliding the license into her purse. Melanie walked out the door, smiling to herself.

Lloyd picked up his clipboard and yelled, "Thomas Kowalski!" A short man with graying hair stood. His scuffed dress shoes squeaked against the floor as he made his way to Lloyd. His keys shook in his hand.

"Let's proceed."

TIO PANZÓN

I stood there alone just inside the doorway of the hospital floor hall. It was a Saturday, the busiest visiting day, the nurse said to me as a man hurried around me, carrying flowers, and another nurse pushed a cart of covered plates. Lunch.

"I am here to see . . . " I started in my broken Spanish to the nurse next to me. Her nametag read *Adelina*. She wore a little pink paper hat.

"You're Elizabeth, yes? Your Uncle Esteban told me you would arrive today. Let me show you where he is," she said in Spanish. She walked toward the big round desk in the center of the hall, signaling for me to follow her.

The hospital was only half finished and composed of a labyrinth of halls. Only a few halls even had roofs, which meant the air was humid and damp. There wasn't enough money to complete the building. There was barely enough money to take care of the patients. As I walked behind Adelina, I looked up at a clear blue sky.

"You are not from around here, your uncle says."

"No. I am from Chicago," I said, watching her small feet take long strides. The rooms we passed by had no doors. I glanced in each one as I followed behind her, catching a glimpse of mismatched tiles and beds framed with steel bars.

"Ah, Chicago," she said, pronouncing Chicago with a hard *ch*. "Is this your first time in El Salvador?"

"Yes. I always wanted to come, but not for a reason like this," I said. She didn't answer, and I wasn't sure if it was because she was thinking of how it must be to fly three thousand miles to see someone for the last time, or because my Spanish was so bad.

Adelina stopped in front of a room and waved through the doorway.

"He's right inside in the corner bed. I have to tell you the same thing I tell all families going through this: please don't get upset when you see him. It will only upset him more. He doesn't look like the last time you saw him."

"I haven't seen him in fifteen years," I said, The last time I had seen him, he and my Tía Diana were leaving Chicago to move back to El

Salvador. Tía Diana had hoped the move, being
back in his homeland, would help Tío Esteban
quit drinking. We had said goodbye at the airport
bar. *Have a beer with me. Last one until you come and
visit.* And I did.

"You know your uncle has lost a leg, yes? We
had to remove it last week. The diabetes was too
advanced to save it, what with the gangrene."

I nodded. Mom cried as she told me her only
brother was dying, that I should have gone to
see him sooner and needed to go now, in case I
never got the chance. I tried not to think about
Tío Esteban's leg, or of him, unable to walk, his
body ripe with pain.

"What you may not know, because we just
told him this morning, is that we need to remove
his other leg, too. It's also infected," The nurse
paused. "He didn't call anyone after we told him.
He said there is no one left to visit him."

I walked in. The room was square, with a
line of narrow beds bordering the far wall, some
empty, some with men that I was too afraid to
look at. There was no roof over the room; the sky
above was the bluest I'd ever seen. I wondered
if the hospital staff placed the patients that were
dying into the roofless rooms, so they could enjoy the sky before they went.

The smell of urine was overwhelming. There were buckets next to each bed, and some were filled partially with piss and shit. My instinct was to cover my nose, but I didn't want to be rude. I didn't want the patients or nurses to think I was judging them.

Cautiously, I looked at the beds. Some of the men were so still I was afraid they were already dead, but then I would see the slight flutter of their breath stir the hairs of their mustaches, or their nostrils moving faintly. There was a man with half his head wrapped in bandages, and there were drops of dried blood on his face. I looked away and followed the nurse to my Tío Esteban, who was lying in a bed with empty beds on either side of him.

"Elizabeth!" he said when he saw me. He smiled and struggled to sit up.

"Tío, I got it." I took the two flat pillows behind him and folded them over, so he could rest against them.

"Thank you, mija. You look wonderful. It's so wonderful to have you here." A single white sheet was tucked under his bare arms. I glanced at the sheet, at the empty space where one leg should have been, and then at the mound that was the leg he was about to lose.

When I was a young kid, hiding my crook-ed-toothed smile with my hands, Tío Esteban would chase the neighborhood kids by barking and making his hands into claws. His legs were strong from playing soccer, and he could run fast. The kids laughed and he laughed. Now he was lying on a bed in a country so far from that neighborhood. Now he couldn't even stand.

Nurses in their off-white uniforms moved around us in a dance that took them from one side of the room to the other. Clearly, the stench no longer affected them. They bent to pick up the buckets, a few at a time, as if they were filled with water. I wondered when they were going to come and clean out Tío's. How could he lie next to a bucket of his own shit everyday, and have any hope that he would ever get better?

"Sit down," he said, but the bed he was on was too narrow. His skin was darker than I re-membered, and he had many more wrinkles on his face. He had also lost all of his hair.

"I'm ok standing, Tío. I just sat on a plane for so long. How are you?"

I immediately regretted asking him. He was sixty years old and dying. He had lost one leg and had just found out he would lose the other. *That* was how he was doing.

"I'm fine, mija. I can see you are a little upset. You have always been so nervous. Here. Sit right here." He patted the bed next to him. "Who says losing a leg is a bad thing? When you're in a bed this small, it makes room for visitors to sit down." He laughed.

I couldn't help it; I laughed, too. He always had the ability to do that. When my dad died I thought I would never smile again, but Tío Esteban was the first one to make it happen. A couple of months after Dad was gone, Tío showed up at my house.

"Let's go to the carnival," he said.

Dad had taken me every year when the carnival was in town. We'd go on the rides and Mom would wave at us from the sidelines because the rides made her nauseous. I had known the carnival was back in town, but I didn't much feel like going.

"Your dad never let you miss it. Let's go and have fun. He would want you too."

He was right. As Tío Esteban careened around on the Tilt-a-Whirl, I thought I felt Dad smiling at us.

I sat on the bed, feeling the stiff mattress beneath me. He put his hand on mine and I saw it was covered with brown spots. I stared at his

hand because I didn't want to really look at his
face. I didn't want to see in it the things that
had changed. I didn't want to leave the hospital and remember him differently than when I
had arrived.

"You were only fifteen the last time I saw you.
You haven't really changed," he said.

"Man, I hope I have," I said, making him
laugh. A nurse came by and smiled at us. She
took the bucket next to his bed with her.

He was very thin. Back in Chicago, my cousins and I use to call him Tio Panzón, the uncle
with the big stomach. He liked the nickname.
Said he was proud that his belly was full of beer
and delicious home cooking.

"So, your mom came to see me last month.
What a scene." He shook his head.

"She told me that when she saw you she
screamed. I had hoped it was in her head." Mom
could be dramatic. She didn't mean it in a mean
way, but it could be embarrassing at times.

"She screamed so loud that the guy who had
just died over in that bed over there was shocked
back to life."

"Tio Goofball," I said.

"So, you're a big time doctor now?" he smiled
and his eyes glimmered. He and Tía Diana never

had children. I think they considered their nieces and nephews the next closest thing. "I wouldn't call it big time, Tío. I'm a veterinarian at a small family-owned clinic."

"You're happy, no? Since you were little that's all you ever wanted to be."

"I am very happy." I paused. "Tío, I'm so sorry I didn't come sooner. With school and then working and other things, I just thought I'd have more time. That we'd have more time." I turned away from him and stared at the empty bed.

"Remember when your Tía Diana died?"

"Yes. I'm sorry I wasn't here for that, either." I started to cry.

"But you were, Elizabeth. You called me. You called me at night when you knew I wouldn't be sleeping anyway because I couldn't, not with her gone. You sent letters, too. You were there for me."

We were silent. He closed his eyes for a bit, and I could tell he was tired. The nurse came back with an empty bucket, then hurried away, probably to clean another. I looked around; the room had filled with visitors. There was someone sitting at nearly every bed. The room felt more humid, and it seemed to be filling with more flies.

After Tía Diana and Tío Esteban moved back to El Salvador, Tía Diana called Mom to tell her Tío Esteban was doing much better. He was drinking less. But then a few years later, Tía Diana had a stroke and died. And Tío Esteban went back to drinking, and refusing to take his insulin. And now he was here.

Tio Esteban slept quietly next to me. I wasn't sure how he could, what with the heat, and the sheet, and the other patients groaning, and their visitors talking loudly, and the nurses chattering and cleaning.

I wished I could take him away, back to the States. I could set him up in a room of his own with air conditioning and nurses with call buttons, and his own bathroom, and a roof, but he had already told Mom that he was going to die in his homeland, where he had met his wife, and where she had died, so he could be buried next to her.

"I'm sorry," Tío Esteban grumbled as he began to wake up.

"That's ok. I know you're tired." I forced a smile and squeezed his hand.

His eyes began to well up, and he turned away. "Because I didn't listen," he said. "Because I got myself in this place."

I didn't know what to say. When I started
to cry, he wiped my eyes and motioned for me
to put my head on his chest. We lay like this
until the muffled conversations, and the cries,
and squeaking of the nurses' shoes grew quiet
again, and all that was left for me to hear was
his breathing.

I saw Tío Esteban every day for the next three
days. After the second amputation procedure,
I stayed at his bedside, even though he wasn't
awake much. I stared at the emptiness on the
bed and wondered how he would feel when he
woke up.

Over the next two days, we talked about our
memories from Chicago. He told me Tía Diana
was the most beautiful woman he had ever seen.

"Do you have someone special back home?"
his eyes looked more alert than they had been.

"Yes. Ryan. But we're just close friends."
I smiled.

"Don't be so nervous, Elizabeth. See if there
is something Ryan feels too. A lot of us men
won't make the first move when we really care
for someone. Thank God, your Tía Diana asked
me out to the beach. That day was so beautiful.
Imagine how I would be without her."

On my last visit, he looked sad. He didn't hide his tears this time.

"I'm going to miss you," he said. I wiped his tears away.

Right before I said my last goodbye, he said, "Did you hear? They are finally going to put a roof over this place."

"Well, that is good," I said.

"No. I like being able to look at the sky. If they put the roof up, I will never see the outside again."

Two months later, Mom called to tell me Tío Esteban had died. I imagined him as Tío Panzón with his big belly, standing on two strong legs. I imagined him on the beach, his arm around Tía Diana, the ocean waves rolling in at their feet, smiling and looking at up at the sky.

BLIND GUY

Being inside that candy shop every day of the
year was like being inside a Fruit Loops cereal
box. Fucking colors everywhere, so many shades
and hues you couldn't even count 'em. All of it
just sugar.

On one side of the store, there were chocolate bars of all kinds and sizes, filled with nuts
or caramel or fudge. Chocolate bunnies with
gooey marshmallow filling chocolate hearts,
white chocolate buttons, chocolate pops covered
in hard strawberry candy, and bars with swirls
of white and dark chocolate. There were choco-
lates in yellow boxes that were supposed to look
fancy, but looked cheap as hell. Those sold most
on Valentine's Day. And then there was the glass
counter that I stood behind all day. Below the
countertop were more shelves filled with more
open bins of candy. The good stuff: gummy bears,
gummy worms, gummy fish, sour raspberry

belts, sour blueberry belts, sour apple balls, sour cherry balls, and even some five-flavor sour belts of every color of the rainbow. We had licorice and cotton candy and more jellybeans than could fit into a semi. The whole store was an explosion of sweets and colors.

It gave me a headache, sometimes. All the joy in the place. But it wasn't so bad.

Those kids loved it, of course, even though their teeth were wrecked from sucking too much sugar, from biting too hard into jawbreakers. All of them had cavities.

The brats knew to call me Mr. Murray. No "Daniel," no "mister," no "Hey, Murray." I wouldn't sell them even an ounce of candy if they called me anything else. Seeing that I was the nearest candy shop within a mile radius, and seeing that I was just right across the street from their elementary school, they did what I asked. They called me Mr. Murray, but at first they called me "That blind guy."

When my older brother got too sick to keep the shop up, I offered to help. I wasn't doing anything since my retirement, anyway. I mostly just sat on my couch all day. It was all I wanted to do after four marriages and four divorces and working every day of my life.

George sat me down in his living room on his white couch. "Watch out for The Octopus," he said, then proceeded to cough into his handkerchief. He and Mabel were taking care of their grandkids whose parents were too high to take care of their own. In another room, Mabel was yelling at them all about something.

"The Octopus?"

"The Octopus is this kid that comes into the store. The Octopus needs to be stopped. His name is Jeremy Goland. He lives in the house with the mismatched shutters over on Sacramento Avenue with the hot mom whose tits are like submarines. Know her? Jeremy's kind of fat and he has the blondest curliest hair. So blonde it might as well be white. That's how you'll know it's him. That kid. He steals. The candy's there one minute, and then the next all that's left are the wrappers."

After a couple of grunts, a few coughs, he continued.

"He's a little stealing bastard, that Jeremy Goland. All the business owners in the neighborhood call him The Octopus because he has more hands than a casino on the Vegas strip. I've never caught him. One time, I thought I saw him put some gumballs in his pants pockets and I yelled,

'You!' I went over and hit him at the hip with one of those long candy straws and asked him to empty his pockets. And you know what he did? He just smiled. Wasn't scared. He turned out his pockets and all he had in there were pebbles and lint! All I know is after he left there was still was gum missing.

"You need to catch him, you hear? Beat it out of him if you have to. Bribe the other kids to tell. You've got one advantage: them kids have never seen you before."

And that gave me an idea.

My first day at the shop, I put on some big sunglasses with thick rims. You couldn't see my eyes through the lenses, but from my end, I could see everything. They were like those one-way mirrors they have in ladies' changing rooms to catch broads stealing stuff. That's what my second wife Dolores used to tell me anyway, before she took her kid and left.

Anyway, I stood behind the counter, glasses on, holding a broomstick, the plastic handcuffs I got at the general store tucked in my back pocket. I even got a dog, but the shelter didn't have those labs or any seeing-eye canine, so I ended up with this mutt with huge bat ears. I mean, he wasn't really supposed to lead me around anyway and I could have got along with just a cane, but I thought a dog would add to the dramatic effect. I learned about dramatic effect in 10th grade. I was Romeo in the school play.

The bell over the front door didn't ring all day, except for when this young man came in to ask for directions. I told him how could I know where he should go if I couldn't see? I saw him shake his head in apology, but if I were really blind would that have mattered? He scurried out, *a sorry*, and the door shut behind him.

Three o'clock came and I could hear the bell ringing from the school and the noise of the brats leaving together, like one big fucking choir being released from the gates of heaven or hell, depending on how you looked at it.

Some little red-headed girl entered right away, waved her hand in front of me and said, "I got a chocolate bar, mister."

"Mr. Murray," I said. "And don't try to jip me. I know which coins are which by just feeling them."

She left the exact change on the counter. I played the blind man for the couple of hours. Not one of those kids stole from me or gave me less money than they should have. Some kids waved their hands in front of my face, one kid with a missing tooth stuck out his slimy little tongue, and a little girl with crooked pigtails picked her nose and left what she found under my counter. Other than that, no Octopus.

At six o'clock, I started closing shop when I heard the bell and turned. Swaggering into the shop was a fat kid with almost white hair and a sneer on his face. It was The Octopus.

"Hello? Who's there?" I called, suddenly remembering I couldn't see. Kennedy—that's what I named the mutt—was on a leash next to my feet, asleep.

"I said, 'who's there?'" I called again, pretending to sound alarmed. I moved my head whenever I heard the floor creak. The Octopus smiled wickedly, revealing teeth like a piranha. He was built like a van, but he couldn't have been more than ten, and he moved through the store as graceful as a ballerina.

He didn't say anything as he picked up one lollipop and then put it back, as he snatched up some chocolate and then put it back. When he came closer to me, waving his hand in front of my face, I saw there a Ring Pop on his finger that he hadn't paid for. I hadn't even noticed him put it on. He stuck out his tongue and licked the pop right in front of me.

He was good all right, this kid. But today was the day. The Octopus was caught.

I didn't say anything. I stood there trying to shake Kennedy's leash to wake him up, so he might at least stop snoring and look like a tough seeing-eye dog or whatnot. But instead the damn dog rolled on his back, his little paws fluttering like he was having a bad dream.

I was just about to announce that I was going to call the cops or, better yet, give me him a smack to show him that you ain't supposed to take nothing that don't belong to you, but then he whistled at Kennedy. Kennedy woke up, walked around to the other side of the counter, the leash trailing like a line in the sand, and sat splat down in front of the kid.

The Octopus smiled, bent on one knee and reached for Kennedy, and I was about to say that the dog ain't ready for no commitment when his shirt moved just so and I saw one hell of a bruise on his neck. It wasn't the kind of bruise you got playing ball or rough housing with your pals. I knew that kind of bruise. I didn't say anything as he pet Kennedy, who started smacking his tail against the floor. And then I noticed another bruise on his upper arm. This one was fading to an ugly yellow color.

My pops gave me a bruise like that once. More than once, actually. It always happened when he was all riled up about not having a job or losing a job or getting jipped on a job. *You kids eat too much*, he'd say, and George and I'd get hit with his belt so much our backs shined. My ma tried to stop him once, which didn't end pretty, and George and I told her we could take it. It was better he hit us than our ma.

The sun was starting to head out, and the store was filled with this orange light that made the candy glitter all crazy and shit. The Octopus stopped smiling and gave Kennedy one last pat on the head. He stood up and looked at me like he could see through my sunglasses, even though I knew he couldn't. But what the hell was he looking so hard at my face for?

Finally The Octopus licked his Ring Pop and looked away. Maybe he got a crook in his neck or something. When he started to walk away, I called after him.

"You didn't pay for that."

The Octopus turned and looked at me. "I knew you could see, mister."

"Mr. *Murray*."

The Octopus put his hand without the Ring Pop in his pants pocket. "Your dog ain't no seeing eye dog. He looks old and little. What's his name?"

"Kennedy. And don't go on trying to change the subject now. You still ain't paid for that candy ring you got on your hand."

"I don't have the money."

"So why did you take it then?"

He shrugged.

"Stealing is wrong, kid. Didn't your parents ever tell you that?" The sun was almost gone. The store was getting dark, especially from behind my sunglasses.

"I think you can take off the glasses now," he said.

I had no reason to keep them on, so I snatched them off. "So, how you gonna pay?"

"What if I don't? What you gonna do? Chase me down the street? You'd run out of breath before you even reach the door," he said.

I thought about turning on the lights, but I didn't want to move because I knew he'd run. And he was right. I wouldn't make it to the door.

"Your old man smacks you around?" I grabbed the stool next to me and sat down. I was now more at his level.

"What?"

"Don't go acting like you don't hear me, now.

You tell me, and you don't have to pay me for that candy ring, or any of the other candy you took before today. How does that sound?"

The Octopus exhaled. From the floor, Kennedy started snoring again.

"Well?"

He looked away. "Sometimes."

"I'm going to turn on the lights," I said, and reached around to hit the switch. I squinted at him as my eyes adjusted and he seemed smaller.

"Sometimes, huh?"

"Yeah. Sometimes."

"You know, my old man sometimes hit me too. You see this scar here by my ear? Before my face got all saggy and shit, you could really see it. I used to tell people I got it in 'Nam, but really it was my old man. Pure fist. Bam. Opened up my face where I couldn't see with all the blood there. Eight or nine stitches."

"Why'd he do that?"

"Hell, I think I breathed or sneezed or something. Look, I know how you feel. You got no control. He does what he wants and you wanna do the same when you ain't home. Trust me kid, that's not the way to go. Only makes it worse." I paused, wondering what he was thinking. "A week after I left for 'Nam, he drove straight drunk into a fucking pole. Head nearly cut off."

He looked at me for a second and then licked the Ring Pop. "Whatever, old man," he said, and then ran so fast out the store. Kennedy didn't even raise his head till the door slammed shut.

The phone rang. It was George.

"You see that kid I was telling you about today? The Octopus?"

"Jeremy?" I asked.

"Yeah. Give me some good news here. My hip is about to crack."

"He was here. I took care of it."

"Son of a bitch!" George said.

The next day I didn't wear the sunglasses and I let Kennedy off his leash. When the kids came in after school, the kids that had been there the day before looked at me strange.

"I thought you were blind," the nose-picking girl said.

"I've been saved. Now, you gonna buy some candy? And use a tissue, for Gods' sake."

Jeremy didn't come back into the candy shop till a week later. He whistled Kennedy over.

"You're back," I said.

He nodded and pet Kennedy behind the ear.

"My dad's been locked up and ain't coming back. Guess someone called." Jeremy said. Kennedy wagged his tail.

"Things have a way of working out sometimes." I said.

Jeremy nodded, gave Kennedy another pet, and left.

FOSSILS

What a cliché it was for two writers to first kiss between book stacks in the library, but Andrew's eyes were dark and his skin brown and when he smiled I felt light, like I could float away.

What a fucking movie we could make.

After that kiss, we spent the next few months going to readings or bowling with friends or sometimes just lounging by the lake. Then always back to his place for sex. I'd leave before he could ask me to stay over. We had a silent agreement: we weren't exclusive; we each enjoyed our space; we each had walls. It worked.

So I didn't expect it when one night he said, "I love you." I was straddling him, my back arched, my long hair falling down. I didn't stop. I kept going and so did he. I stared at the other side of the room, where the television was on mute.

I didn't know if Andrew wanted me to say it

back. People say things they don't mean during sex all the time.

When we finished and sweaty and our chests were heaving, Andrew and I lay side by side in his bed. He always smelled like toast to me. I liked to joke that I was butter and my body, next to his, melting.

"Do you want to stay over?" he asked.

"Thanks, but not tonight. I have a story I need to figure out."

"One night you'll stay," he said, yawning, and fell asleep. I threw back the covers and began looking for my shoes.

Some people go to church to think about things. Some people go to the bar. But the next morning, I went to the library. I ran my fingers along the book spines as I paced up and down the rows, both hands reaching out, touching them all.

I had never talked to Andrew about Steve, although I think Andrew knew there was someone before him that had left me this way, unable to say that I actually did love him. I felt everything for Andrew that I did for Steve and that was the thing. I thought Steve was it. And then Steve was gone.

I grabbed a book with a green cover that was

sticking out. *Bringing Fossils to Life* was spelled across the cover in black letters above a picture of two fish in thin fractured lines. I rubbed the pages under my fingers like I could read with my skin.

I decided to check out the book, though I didn't think I had any use for it. Maybe I'd show Andrew. Maybe he could use it for one of his stories. I left it on the table next to my bed. It was there next to me as I went to sleep.

The next day, Andrew and I soaked in the first of the summer sun by the lake, my bare legs white against the greenish-blue of the water. His arm cast shadows over mine. He liked to caress the beauty mark under my lip with his fingertips. *This is my favorite*, he'd say before kissing it.

"I love you, Maya. I just want you to know that. You don't have to say it back."

I said nothing and stared over the water. The wind blew my hair into my face. The waves were rolling in heavily, churning the water so I couldn't see through it.

Andrew moved away from me and looked down at the water. "I'm hungry. Want to get some pizza?" He got up before I had a chance to answer.

We ate the pizza at his place, not even waiting for the steam to evaporate. I poured Cholula sauce on my slices from the bottle I kept in is refrigerator. *I've heard of leaving a toothbrush, but hot sauce?* he had joked.

When we finished eating, Andrew said, "I have to write tonight."

"Me too," I nodded. I grabbed my bag and reached for the book with the green cover. "I thought you might want to check this out."

Andrew took the book and felt the cover just as I had.

We made our way to the couch and lay next to each other in silence. His fingertips traced my spine up and down like he was trying to find something in the dark. We both watched the sun crawl across the living room until it was over us, all around us, shining.

MUCH GRATITUDE

To the many people who saw me through this book and heard me eek like a dolphin when it was good and saw me ugly cry when I didn't know if I had anymore to give.

My thesis advisor Joe Meno, Patricia Ann McNair, Randall Albers, Eric May, for their guidance and continued belief and support, and the Columbia College Chicago Fiction Department.

Bonnie Jo Campbell, John McNally, and Mark Protosevich for their inspiration, knowledge, and making me all giddy with their kind words.

Chicago Reader, Hypertext Magazine, Literary Orphans, Chicago Literati, First Ink!ing, Silvertongue—where a number of these stories in some form were previously published.

Victor David Giron, Jacob S. Knabb, Naomi Huffman, Alban Fischer, and to the rest of my amazing Curbside Splendor Family, for this incredible journey.

To my lovelies—Doris Cole, Miriam Mendoza, Adriana Galván, Melanie Galván, and Maggie Ramirez—for being such incredible souls.

My ma who raised three kids on her own. The strongest woman I know.

My sweet dog, Olivia. Who snuggled next to me through my many long hours of writing these stories.

Most of all to my husband, Cesar T. Vargas and daughter, Viviana V. Vargas. My heart and soul are yours.

CYN VARGAS holds an MFA from Columbia College Chicago, and is the recipient of a Ragdale Fellowship and the 2013 Guild Literary Complex Prose Award in Fiction. Cyn was named one of Guild's Literary Complex's 25 Writers to Watch in 2014 and received two top citations in *Glimmer Train*'s Short Story Award for New Writers contest. She is a company member of the award-winning storytelling organization 2nd Story. Her work has appeared in *Chicago Reader*, *Word Riot*, *Literary Orphans*, and elsewhere. She teaches creative writing workshops around Chicago, and can be found online at cynvargas.com.

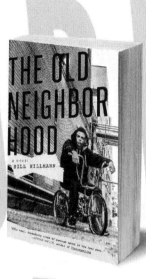

THE OLD NEIGHBORHOOD
A NOVEL BY BILL HILLMANN

"A raucous but soulful account of growing up on the mean streets of Chicago, and the choices kids are forced to make on a daily basis. This cool, incendiary rites of passage novel is the real deal." —IRVINE WELSH, AUTHOR OF *TRAINSPOTTING*

A bright and sensitive teen. Joe Walsh is the youngest in a big. mixed-race Chicago family. After Joe witnesses his heroin-addicted oldest brother commit a brutal gangland murder, his friends and loved ones systematically drag him deeper into a black pit of violence that reaches a bloody impasse when his eldest sister begins dating a rival gang member.

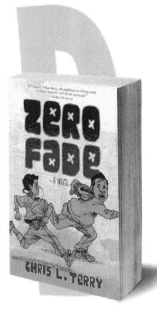

ZERO FADE

A NOVEL BY CHRIS L. TERRY

"Humor, sadness, confusion, joy, revelation. It's all here in Terry's first novel, a novel that is practically carbonated, how it sparkles and burns." —LINDSAY HUNTER, AUTHOR OF *UGLY GIRLS*

Thirteen-year-old Kevin Phifer has a lot to worry about. His father figure, Uncle Paul, is coming out as gay; he can't leave the house without Tyrell throwing a lit Black 'n' Mild at him; Demetric at school has the best last-year-fly-gear and the attention of orange-haired Aisha; his mother Sheila and his nerdy best friend David have both found romance; his big sister Laura won't talk to him now that she's in high school; and to top it off, he's grounded.

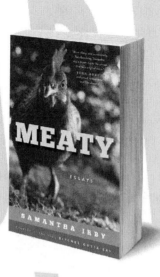

MEATY
ESSAYS BY SAMANTHA IRBY

*"Raunchy, funny and vivid . . . Those faint of heart beware . . .
strap in and get ready for a roller-coaster ride to remember."*
—*KIRKUS REVIEWS*

Samantha Irby explodes onto the page with essays about laughing
her way through a life of failed relationships, taco feasts, bouts with
Crohn's Disease, and more. Written with the same scathing wit and
poignant bluntness readers of her riotous blog have come to expect,
Meaty takes on subjects both high and low—from why she can't
be mad at Lena Dunham, to the anguish of growing up with a sick
mother, to why she wants to write your mom's Match.com profile.

LET GO AND GO ON AND ON

A NOVEL BY TIM KINSELLA

*"I give Kinsella a five thousand star review for launching me
deep into an alternate universe somewhere between fiction
of the most intimate and biography of the most compelling."*

—DEVENDRA BANHART

In *Let Go and Go On and On* the story of obscure actress Laurie Bird
is told in a second-person narrative, blurring what little is known of
her actual biography with her roles as a drifter in *Two Lane Blacktop*,
a champion's wife in *Cockfighter*, and an aging rock star's girlfriend
in *Annie Hall*. Kinsella explores our endless fascination with the
Hollywood machine and the weirdness that is celebrity culture.

"Cyn Vargas brings her readers a whole world of unforgettable women, old and young, tough and getting tougher. Her narrators must continually negotiate with the tragedy, cruelty, and sweetness of their ever-changing lives, against the twin landscapes of America and Central America. In these fresh, sensual stories, Vargas bravely explores family, friendship and irreconcilable loss, and she will break your heart nicely."

—**BONNIE JO CAMPBELL**, author of
Once Upon a River

"First: I flat-out love this book. I do. Second: I love that Cyn Vargas is in the world to have written this book. She's a mischievously good writer who lures you in with her humor and then breaks your heart in these generous and compelling stories about good people who are often haunted by what's missing in their lives. Third: If you are reading this, start reaching for your credit card. I want you to buy this book. It'll be the best decision you've made in a long, long time. Trust me."

—**JOHN MCNALLY**, author of
After the Workshop

"It's rare for stories about childhood, friendship, the elderly, marriage, family secrets, and loneliness and longing to be told with quiet beauty and grace, but the stories in *On the Way* accomplish just that. Cyn Vargas approaches her characters with a delicate and loving hand, always honest, sometimes angry, but never judgmental. Just like how we approach the people we love—whether we're bound to them by blood or by choice.

— **MARK PROTOSEVICH**, screenwriter, *I Am Legend*, *Oldboy*, and *The Cell*